THE
Language
OF
Fire

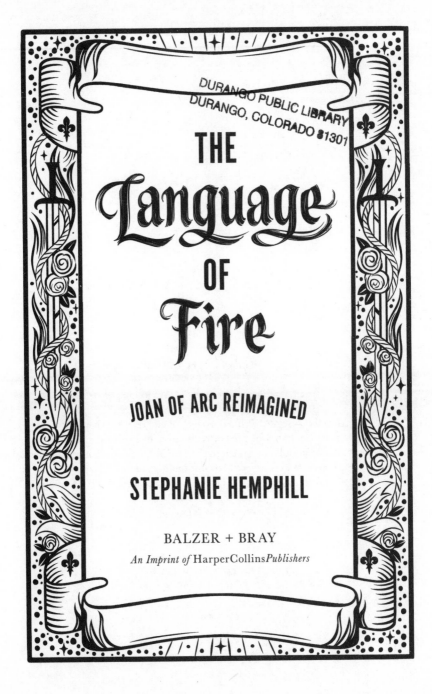

THE
Language
OF
Fire

JOAN OF ARC REIMAGINED

STEPHANIE HEMPHILL

BALZER + BRAY

An Imprint of HarperCollins*Publishers*

Balzer + Bray is an imprint of HarperCollins Publishers.

The Language of Fire: Joan of Arc Reimagined
Copyright © 2019 by Stephanie Hemphill
All rights reserved. Printed in the United States of America.
No part of this book may be used or reproduced in any manner whatsoever
without written permission except in the case of brief quotations embodied
in critical articles and reviews. For information address HarperCollins
Children's Books, a division of HarperCollins Publishers, 195 Broadway,
New York, NY 10007.
www.epicreads.com

ISBN 978-0-06-249011-7

Typography by Jenna Stempel-Lobell
19 20 21 22 23   PC/LSCH   10 9 8 7 6 5 4 3 2 1
❖
First Edition

For those who find the courage to act,
despite their fears.

THE
Language
OF
Fire

"ALL BATTLES
ARE FIRST
WON OR LOST,
IN THE MIND."
-JEHANNE D'ARC

The Hundred Years' War officially began in 1337
and ended in 1453, but periodic fighting over
English holdings in France date back to
the twelfth century. A conflict between England
and France over the succession to the French crown,
the Hundred Years' War was fought almost exclusively
on French soil over French lands.

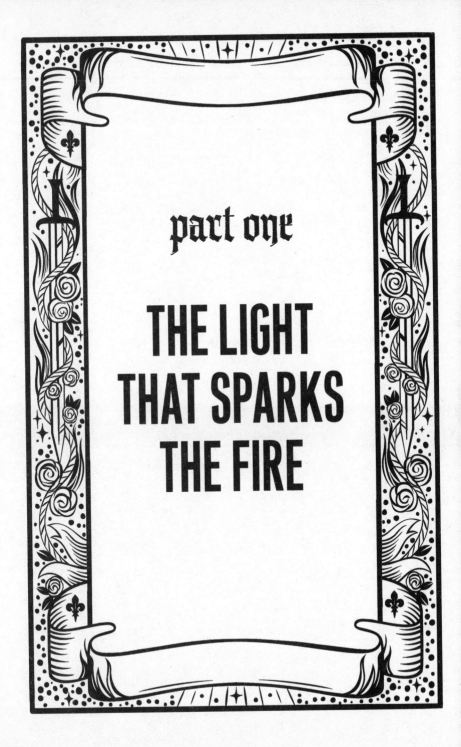

part one

THE LIGHT THAT SPARKS THE FIRE

ON FIRE

May 30, 1431

When they ignite my stake
I expect the fire
to speak—
through so many dreams
flames have beckoned me
like a drum.

After hearing and heeding His voice,
I thought at the end
God might call out
my name.
I hoped angels
would sing and shelter me
with wings of comfort.

But this blaze roars
without consolation,
without words.

Perhaps I am beyond
words now.

Even the crowd,
who howled like starving dogs
before my pyre was lit,
stands solemn and silent.

The only sound
piercing the smoky air
is the scream of a girl
named Jehanne.
But
I became so much more.

THIRTEEN AND FUMBLING

1425

I have always been a duck
fumbling in a flock of geese.
But I try to fit in.

I learn to sew and spin,
to craft soap from sheep's tallow,
to tend, cook, thresh, and plow.
Like my older sister, Catherine,
I'm taught all my mother's chores.

I want to fit in
like my friends
Hauviette and Isabellette.
I try to think like they do
about which boy is best,
but I find this game more boring
than soap.

Why should I coo
about boys who tease me
when I outrun them in a race?
Colin and Marc call me strange,
Jehanne with lanky bird legs.

My sister says teasing
means they like me.
But I know their words
are wasps, not honey,
aimed to wound me
just because I'd rather run
than watch.

Most days I feel like
I don't fit the sleeves
of my own dress.

How am I to belong?

NOTHING TO DO

"Did you ever wish
to be something
besides a wife and mother?"

Mengette looks at me
as though my teeth
just fell out of my mouth.
"Oh, you mean like a nun?
No, not me. Not even
if I lost my dear Collot.
But I wouldn't hope
for that, cousin. Your father
wants you to marry a man,
not the church."

I know she's right,
but there's a restless
thrumming in my chest,
as if boredom and this little village
might swallow me whole.

The noon chapel bells toll.
I close my eyes and imagine
the chimes call forth
a great army of angels
riding valiant white steeds,
and I am among them.

"My mother made a pilgrimage
to Rome when she was a girl.
Maybe I can do that too?"

"Don't be ridiculous, Jehanne.
France is at war.
That's too dangerous a trip for a man,
let alone a girl from Lorraine.
Just be content as you are."

I turn away from Mengette.

The sun hides behind
a patch of billowy clouds
as the bells fall silent.

Even if I can't change
the direction of the wind,
why must I agree
that foul air smells sweet?

AGAINST THE GRAIN

It's not as if I ask to be
the girl on the margins,
the one going left
where others turn right.

Mother says I'm just sensitive.
I see and hear things
when others are blind and deaf.

But sometimes I wish
my ears would stay closed.
When I overhear my brother Jean say,
"Jehanne is so odd. Perhaps
something's wrong with her,"
I wish I could unhear those words.

HISTORY OF A COUNTRY DIVIDED

For as long as
cattle have grazed our fields,
and church bells tolled
at midday meal,
France has been fighting
over who should rule our nation.

Generations of warfare
have divided my country
into a patchwork quilt
of loyalty.

Armagnacs who support the dauphin
stand on one side of the battlefield,
and French Burgundians
who ally with the English
occupy the other.

My family lives
at the edge of this conflict,
hundreds of miles from Paris
and even farther from Chinon,
where the dauphin Charles resides.
Our village, Domrémy,
nestles inside the only territory
of Armagnac support
in the northeast.

In constant combat
with our Burgundian neighbors,
lands are lost and gained
as rapidly as tides rise in a flood.
But somehow
my family always rebuilds.

It's the bruised and broken
French countryside
whose suffering knows no end.

SAFER THAN MOST

Our family has always been set apart.
We live in a stone house,
not a wooden one like everyone else.
It doesn't burn
when English soldiers
ravage our village like wolves.

My father, Jacques d'Arc,
is dean of Domrémy,
tallies the tax money.
Father says that makes us more
responsible for our country and others.
We give shelter to travelers, alms to the poor,
because we can.

But even at a safe retreat
from the marauding and the battles,
with the village's pigs corralled
behind a fortress on the River Meuse,
I smell fire.

Ashes shower from the sky,
blot out the sun,
and blacken my home
in a relentless rain of dirt.

FIRE

It's always the same dream—

English soldiers
brandishing angry torches.
The wooden beams
of our barn ignite
into a cage of flames.
And I'm trapped in the rafters.

I scream until my lungs explode,
but no one hears me.
No one arrives to help.

The devilish heat licks my boots,
kindles my hair.
My dress blooms
into a blazing carpet.

The ground beneath the barn
opens as a wound,
and I'm swallowed
straight to hell.

I wake in wild sweats.
What does this dream mean?

MY FRIEND

Hauviette and I have been friends
since we could crawl.
She grabs my hand
and twirls me into a dance,
whistles back at
a cackling woodpecker
as she braids narcissi
into my hair.
She tells me I should smile more,
that it makes me more attractive.
Boys don't like girls
to always be so serious.

Nothing ever troubles Hauviette.
Not the enemy threatening us
across the river,
not the lack of grain
in her father's silo,
not her sinful behavior
flirting with my brother Jean

during yesterday's mass,
and certainly
not the staidness
of a woman's place
in village life.

Sometimes I envy her.
Sometimes
I want to shake her
from her bliss
and slumber.

But I wonder:
Could I wake her
even if I tried?

BEING A GIRL

If I could stay a girl forever,
that would be fine.
There is liberty
in not being a wife or mother.
But growing into a woman,
I want no part of that.

It's like our crops
when they die.
You produce fruit,
then wither away.

My sister Catherine
is a woman today,
and she and Mother
celebrate it.

I want to stay young
and pure and free,
unstained by the sin of Eve.

Mother and Catherine
laugh that I will
change my mind
in a few years,
but I know better.

MY THREE BROTHERS

Jacquemin is my eldest sibling
and my father's favorite.
He will soon be married
and move to Vouthon,
where Mother was born.
He is kind to me,
but he worries more
than all the villagers in Domrémy
put together.
I tell Jacquemin
if he prayed more often,
he might not look always
over his shoulder.
My brother sees clouds threatening storms
but misses the beauty of the rain.

Even though we share the same name,
my other older brother, Jean,
and I are nothing alike.
Jean believes that he is the best

at everything. He never fears loss.
My friends find him handsome,
but I think he's rude.
Jean forgets
to kick the mud off his boots
before he enters the house.
He just expects his mess
will be tended by others.

Pierre is the baby
of the family
and wild as a boar.
Always in motion,
he uses his fists
before his mind.
Only a year younger
than me in age,
yet he and I stand
a decade of wisdom
apart.

Not one
of my three brothers
realizes how fortunate
he is to be a boy.

ALONE

In the pasture beyond our farm
I hide under the high grass and spy.
Hauviette and my brother Jean
stand beside each other,
so close a breath
could not fit between them.

I wonder what that feels like,
to have someone look at you
the way Jean stares at my friend,
as though Hauviette alone exists.
They're in a meadow
rich with animals, trees, sunlight—
yet she is all to him.

I will know the same feeling
my sister promises
when the time is right.
But sometimes I worry
that like my brother said,

something is wrong with me
and I'll never understand
that kind of love.
Even worse, maybe
I don't care.

ONE GIRL'S PRAYER

Sometimes I wish
I could be like my sister and friends,
lining a trousseau
with the joy and anticipation
of Christmas morn.
Sometimes I wish
I could be like my brothers,
reckless as cattle run astray
yet able to own property
and speak my mind.

I feel like a book
that will never be read.
I contain wisdom,
but no one will open me
to discover it.
And I'll never
have the schooling
to read it myself.

MY THIRTEENTH SUMMER

1425

After a morning tilling the field
with my brothers,
I escape to my father's garden.

Flowers stretch toward the clouds,
humming with insects and color.
Everything smells golden and round.

I feel like I belong here.
Roses and radishes don't judge—
they only radiate God's love.

Something stirs in the corner,
a rustling of leaves,
a great flash of light—
but when I look,
I find nothing, no one.

Jehanne,
a voice calls out
clear as a church bell.

"Who's there?"

Jehanne!
someone cries,
and the sky flares
as if it's lit
by a thousand suns.

I search every flower bed,
every inch of soil,
but I'm alone.

Jehanne,
I hear again.

"Who speaks to me?
Where are you?"

I get no response.

NOTHING TO SPEAK ABOUT

"You look pale, Jehanne,"
Mother says, and places
her hand on my temple.
"Do you feel well?"

I resist pushing away
her hand.

I'm not sure
what just happened
in the garden
or what's been stirring
inside me lately, bubbling over
like an untended broth,
but it's probably best
not to speak about it.
I fear no one, not even
my mother, would understand.

I must have imagined
someone called my name,
but it sounded very real.

JUST BEFORE SUPPER

Father blusters into the house.
"The Burgundian
governor-general of Barrois
attacked Sermaize."

Mother stumbles,
and my sister and I
steady her into a chair.

Father removes his hat
and lowers his voice.
"Collot Turlot was killed."

I bite the inside
of my cheek.
Collot is
my cousin Mengette's husband
and served as an Armagnac soldier.

My father's eyes avoid everyone.
They settle instead on the dusty floor.

Tears streak my mother's face.
She makes no attempt
to wipe them away,
as if she wishes to feel drenched
in her suffering.

Father sighs.
"When our enemy approaches,
we French open our gates."

My brother Jean slaps
the table and says loudly,
"The dauphin should take up the fight!
Why does he do nothing?"

"I suppose warfare is best left
to kings and soldiers.
We are farmers and herdsmen.
What do we know?"
Father dabs the sweat off his brow.

"You are the dean of Domrémy,
Father. You know as much
as anyone about what goes on,"
my brother Jacquemin offers.

My father pats Jacquemin's back.
He slides into his chair
and reaches for his bowl.
"What do I smell,
mutton and barley?"

Still weeping, Mother nods.

I feel like knocking over the table.
Why do we French do nothing?
How can my father not wish to act?
I think the English have poked
cet ours dormant, this sleeping bear,
one too many times. I blurt out,
"Someone needs to fight back!"

Even though my words mimic
my brother Jean's,
around the room eyes bulge
larger than a family of toads'.
I have spoken outside my scope,
not at all in the manner of a girl.
My family sits silent, uncomfortably still,
for many heartbeats.

Father snaps at me,
"Bless the food, Jehanne."

My throat clenches like a fist.
Still I close my eyes and pray,
"Bless us, O Lord . . ."

LOST LAMB

Instead of helping Mother
around the house and in the stables
this week, I'm told to tend the sheep.
I fear this may be
some sort of punishment
for my brash behavior the other night,
because as much as I like solitude,
I've never loved this job,
minding the pastures
so none of the flock wander
too far afield.
The day seems to double its length.

I bring my spinning wheel
to busy my hands,
and so I won't fall asleep
on soft pillows of prairie grass.

It's been nearly a week since
I heard my name called in the garden.
I want to believe the voice was real,
but more likely my ears deceived me.

"Stop!" I holler.
"Rascal lamb, come back here!
There are wolves in the woods."
I drop my spinning
and start to chase after the vagrant lamb.
Yet if I run down the one,
I leave the rest of the herd alone.
Do I leave the flock or lose the wanderer?

But because girls
are raised not to act,
just to remain quietly
with the pack,
I do nothing.

CAN ANYTHING CHANGE?

No soldier worth his salt
sits on his hands,
gun stuffed between thighs,
and waits to be attacked.
He is not fool enough
to believe doing nothing
will effect change
in this war,
in the lives of his countrymen.

The English have stolen parts of France,
and we must fight to reclaim
what is rightfully ours,
recover our lost lambs from the woods.

But wars are the work of men—
what of mothers and daughters?
Are we expected to watch
as fields and families

are destroyed,
and do nothing?
Can this truly be God's plan?

PURPOSE

When I feel ready to pummel
Jean and Pierre because, once again,
they left the gate open,
and I had to spend half my morning
chasing down a dozen feisty pigs,
Mother reminds me that
along with the squealing swine
I must seek patience.

I muzzle my lips
as I corral the hogs.
Sometimes my life feels as fixed
as that of the pigs I pen.
Have I no higher purpose
than filling slop trays?

I cross myself and pray
that I may understand my place
and find contentment therein.

In response, the same voice
I heard in the garden tells me:

Jehanne,
you are meant to do something more.

WITHOUT HOPE

Our house staggers
with the weight
of Father's news.

Normandy has fallen
to the English.
Seven thousand killed
at Verneuil.
Five of our men died
for each one of theirs.

My brother Jacquemin
lowers his head.
"The dauphin will resign
completely now."

Father agrees.
"They say the dauphin
no longer believes
he has God's favor."

His words crumble with sorrow
like gravel upon the floor.

I run to Mother.
I dare not speak my mind
as I did the other day.
I see by her quivering lip
that she could not bear it.

"I heard something curious in town,"
my sister, Catherine, says
with a voice so steady it's unnerving.
"Remember that old prophecy
the mystic Marie of Avignon foretold:
that France will be restored
by a virgin from Lorraine
called La Pucelle?"

"What of it?" Jean snips.

"Some think it will soon be made true.
Perhaps if the dauphin Charles were reminded
of the prophecy, he would find hope,"
Catherine offers.

My father kisses Catherine's cheek.
"You are a sweet daughter,
but what the dauphin needs

is a victorious army
to regain his hope."

Of course Father praises
Catherine's words
when he slammed his fist
down upon mine.
Sometimes being the younger daughter
feels like I am a bird
with clipped wings.

The voice from the garden startles me
when it says:

Jehanne, you are the prophecy,
the virgin from Lorraine
who will save France.

I look around to see
if anyone else hears these words,
but I am the only one.

How can that be?
The voice sounds as though
someone stands beside me.

My hold on Mother
grows tighter than a noose.
Have I lost my wits?

NO SLEEP FOR THE CONFLICTED

I lie near the hearth tonight
because I offered my bed
to a weary traveler
who needs its comfort
more than I do.
I toss right, roll left,
but I can't find a position to sleep.

I can't stop questioning
whether the voice I heard
spoke the truth.
Could I be the girl of the prophecy
who will save France?

Or perhaps I imagined those words
because I was jealous
that Father praised Catherine?

The main fire dies,
so I jump up to restore it.
As I move toward the chimney,
the flames blaze up
in a fiery dragon's tongue.
Terrified, I search for a bucket of water.

The fire grows stronger. I need help.
But before I can jostle anyone awake,
the firelight envelops me,
wraps me in a blanket
of the softest down.

Blazes swirl around the room,
setting alight pots, chairs,
my father's cloak.
All the furniture glows like candles.

And then, as though called to order,
the flames disappear.
They leave not a trace of ash or ember.

A single radiant light
shines above me
like a sky of only stars.

As I bask in the beam,
the voice only I can hear
confirms last night's premonition.
It tells me:

Do not doubt this, Jehanne.
You are the girl from the old prophecy.
You will be called La Pucelle.
You will lead an army.
And you will save France.

It's clear to me now
who speaks inside my head—
it must be God.

DOUBT

I was convinced last night
that the voice I heard was God,
but today doubt creeps
into my mind
like a long afternoon shadow.

I am just a lowly peasant girl.
Who am I to be chosen
to save France?
The idea is surely folly
fueled by my longing
to be more than I am.

But then again,
what if the voice
I heard is indeed God,
and I fail to do
what he asks of me?
It would be a grave sin
to disobey God.

My mind whirls
like dust clouds in a storm.

My friends dance and sing,
throwing grass in a silly game.
Hauviette calls to me,
but I don't know
what to say to her.
All my words
trap inside my head.
I wave hello but walk alone.

My only place of sanctuary
is the Saint-Rémy village church.
Crystal light breaks
through slats in the roof,
warms and comforts me from above.
On my knees in the chapel
I close my eyes and pray.
I touch the floor,
the wood of the bench,
and feel balance,
forget the dizziness of the world.
And when I gaze up at the cross,
I know
sure as the bell tolls,
the horse whinnies,
and the stars crowd the midnight moon,

that God speaks to me
and I must, and I will,
do as He commands.

FULFILLING THE PROPHECY

1426

Over time I begin to accept
that I am the girl
of the old prophecy.
But if so,
what should I do?

I bite my nails
and tread unending circles.
Why didn't the voice give me
better direction?

Fulfilling a prophecy
feels more overwhelming
than plowing a field
with a fork.

I suppose God would, at minimum,
require that I continue to:
be good
be pious

and go to church often,
but what else?

My little brother, Pierre,
and his friend Colin
stagger up the road
and interrupt my reverie.

They return from Maxey,
a neighboring town
under Burgundian control.
Black-eyed and trouser-torn,
the boys look like someone
ran over them with an oxcart.

"Can you stitch up this hole
at my knee before Mother sees?"
Pierre asks me.

"Father forbade you to fight."

Pierre rolls his eyes.

"But I'll mend the damage."

He winces as I brush
the hair off his forehead
and reveal a nasty gash.

Pierre pushes away my hand.
"It's nothing."

Colin smiles. "We showed
those Burgundy louts,
pelted them with boulders."

Pierre jumps in.
"He means rocks,
pebbles really.
Besides, they started it.
They're the bad ones."
I catch him glaring at Colin
as I thread my needle.

"When real fighting surrounds us,
why do you play at war?"

Colin spits purposefully
into the dirt. "You're a girl.
You wouldn't understand."

Pierre shrugs.
"We fight or they win."
He examines his pant leg.

Whether or not
Pierre and Colin believe me,
I do understand

their desire to fight back.
Still I counsel, "Little brother,
try to stay out of trouble."

As they run off,
I wonder if I shouldn't
heed my own words.
Is it not headstrong and conceited
to think that I am La Pucelle?
To believe that a girl might save France?

JEAN THE MEAN

I will likely never see
my eldest brother again.
Jacquemin departed this morning
to join his bride in Vouthon,
a town four hundred miles
from Domrémy.
I feel his loss
as if my only hat has blown away
and from now on I must suffer
unprotected in the cold.

I stumble to find footing,
for Jean
becomes the oldest son.

Jean lords his new ascendance
over us all
like a cruel king.
"Father says I am in charge

of the flock, the herds,
and the northern fields."
He orders me and Catherine
to thresh the wheat
and Pierre to round up the cattle,
while Jean covers his face with his cap
and lies down for a nap.

I want to kick the lazy lout
swiftly in the shins.

Catherine pats my arm.
"Father will notice
that Jean shirks his duties,
but it is not our place
to reprimand our brother."

I roll my eyes;
sweet, perfect Catherine,
who always knows the right thing to do.
I follow her to the field
and find a sturdy stick.
Each time I thrash the wheat,
I imagine it is a blow
aimed at my brother.
After an hour of severing
the heads from the stalks,
I calm down.

I must remember who I am,
who I am going to be.
A temperamental girl
cannot be the savior of France.

I fall to my knees
and cross myself.
"Please, God,
grant me patience
and endurance,
and please help Jean
correct the error of his ways."

WHAT ELSE CAN I DO?

Hiding my mission
from my family feels dishonest
and therefore in conflict
with God's teachings.

Yet I dare not tell a soul
I have been chosen by God to save France.
I don't think my family
or anyone else would believe me.
How could they?
I still struggle to believe it myself.

●◆●

I must stitch thrice as fast as
Catherine-the-Immaculate-Mender
to sneak away this afternoon.
And when I do, I have a sinking feeling
Catherine's eyes follow me into the fields.

The sun winks behind a cloud,
and the trees fill with light
like blooming lilies.
I stretch my arms to the sky
and continue my mental list
of what God might demand of me.

As I pray,
two things come into my mind:
be reverent
be humble.

I know what it is to be reverent
and worship God,
I go to mass twice a day now.
But I'm not sure I fully understand
the meaning of humility.

I lie down in the meadowland
beyond our crops
and pluck a single piece of grass.
I turn and study it sideways.
Alone, one blade is so small
it appears insignificant,
but when banded together,
blades create a mighty field.
None of the pieces more, or less,
important than the others.

Perhaps that is humility.

I will try always to remember this.

A SNARE OR A CAGE

Sometimes I feel
like a rabbit being baited
into a snare.
I haven't the skills
to protect myself
from predators,
from the dangers of the night.
I may wish
to hop outside my warren,
but I never truly believed
I would do so.

God calls me
to leave my family's nest
and enter the dark forest.

Yet if my father knew of my plans,
he would cage me in the kitchen.
I would not feel sunlight

on my back until I exchanged
marriage vows.

And the truth is
I am lured
by more than God's voice
into the greater world.

I dreamed of the forest,
of leaving my home,
well before He spoke to me.

Still, what if my first leap
is my last?

WHERE HAVE YOU BEEN?

Catherine stands at the back door,
watching me untangle a burr
from my hair.

"I know you were not
tending the sheep
or threshing the field
or weeding the garden
or doing household chores."

"I was praying,
at church."
I tell a partial fib.

She brushes dirt off my shoulder.
"When I met Marc,
I prayed a lot too."

I shake my head.
"It's not what you think."

Catherine smiles.
"I wish you would know
that you can trust me."
She looks at me
as if we share something
that I know we don't.
She kisses my forehead.

Perhaps my sister would understand?
But what if she didn't?
"I promise you,
I am doing nothing sinful."

She chuckles as she spins me around
to retie my apron.
"I know that, Jehanne."

"So, you will keep my secret?"

"Of course I will."

THEY ARE COMING

We learn of the English soldiers' approach
miles before any horses' hooves can be heard.
We gather our best linen and dishes,
the church books and cross,
and move what grain, goods, and livestock
we can south to Neufchâteau,
a town with a crumbling castle
but sturdy walls to protect us.

We villagers are saved
from fire and death,
but not from godless thievery.

I stumble over the rubble and loss
we find back in Domrémy.
The enemy raiders weren't satisfied
with some cattle, grain, and coin.
They wanted to consume all.

A silent fury ignites inside me.
It spreads through my veins
like fire sweeping over a field of grain.

SLEEPING WITH FLAMES

Again, fire blazes through my dreams.
The whole village of Domrémy
smolders.

Houses, barns, fields, and stables
crumble to ash and ember.
The surface of the lake is blackened
as though it has been scorched
by dragon's breath.

I scream for help.
No one hears me.
No one sees.
I feels as if I am
the only person who exists.
Everyone else
must have perished in the fire.

Or perhaps
I was always alone.

MY FATHER'S NIGHTMARE

Though he tries to speak in hushed tones,
my father's voice is bold enough
to corral a runaway herd.
Even from across the barn,
I can't help but overhear him.

"If I had the dream only once,
I might have thought nothing of it.
But three times?"
Father unhitches the ox
as Jean and Pierre
pour grain into the trough.
"It's dreadful. Jehanne is among men-at-arms.
She leaves my home to be among soldiers.
She must be a—
I hate to even speak the words.
But she must be a prostitute."

Jean laughs.
"But Father, all Jehanne does
is work and pray.
She never even looks at a boy."

"I know. It seems lunatic,
but please watch her for me."
Father wipes his brow,
then struggles to find these words:
"Do you ever see her around—
men—
around . . . soldiers?"

Both my brothers say, "No!"

Father releases a sigh.
"Good. You have assured me."
He shakes dirt off his boot.
"Still, if I ever believed Jehanne
would do this sinful thing,
I would ask you to drown her.
And if you would not do it,
I would do it myself."

I feel like I have been kicked
unawares by our ox.
My eyes well with tears,
and I cannot breathe.

But my brothers shake their heads.

Pierre says,
"Jehanne is the most virtuous girl
any of us will ever know.
Have no fear, Father."

My lungs remember
how to breathe again.

When my father and brothers
leave the barn,
I remain among the cows.
I have spoken
of my calling to save France
to no one,
and yet Father imagined me
among soldiers.
Even though he misunderstood why,
he saw me among their ranks—
this proves that the prophecy is true,
that I really am La Pucelle.

PRAYER

I feel most at peace
kneeling in a pew,
inside a house devoted to God,
where His presence surrounds me.

Often, I'm the only person at Saint-Rémy
except for Sacristan Drappier.
My brothers say
they ought to move my bed here,
because these days the only time
I'm not in church,
I'm asleep.

I bless myself,
recite the *Paternoster* and the creed,
and pray to the Holy Mother.

I confess at least daily
to cleanse my soul
of the dirt of my hands.

As the sun nears its bedtime
and I hear the call of my mother,
I kneel before the altar.
I don't ask to understand
my holy mission,
but only to be strong enough
to achieve it,
to believe I can do
what's required of me.
Because I don't yet
feel able or worthy.

MY SISTER

When I pause to admire
the glorious day
as we work together
hoeing the garden,
Catherine smiles and says,
"I look up and I see
clouds and sun,
blue sky and rain.
When you look above, Jehanne,
you see the breath of God
and the teardrops of angels.
You hear heaven's song.
It is a special gift."

We may not
call one another friend,
but Catherine
never has an unkind word
for anyone,
and certainly

not for me.
Though we are as different
as wind and water,
she has never made me feel
wrong.

Sometimes I long
to tell her who I am becoming,
for if anyone would believe me,
it would be Catherine.
But for now,
I keep it to myself.

FINDING STRENGTH WITHIN

A tune plays inside me
that others cannot hear,
music that warms me,
fingers and toes.
It echoes between my ears
and rattles around my brain
as church bells toll.
A song entirely my own—
I chant it to myself,
and all things feel possible.

MY REAL TRAINING BEGINS

If I am to be La Pucelle
and save France,
I must do more than pray.
I must attain some battle skills.

Unfortunately, I have no example
of how to be a virtuous warrior.
French troops
have yet to ride through Domrémy.

The only soldiers
I have known
I wouldn't care to lead.
English and Burgundian soldiers
laugh as they burn
our houses and farms.
Snakes that lurk just below
the surface of the water,
they are evil creatures
eager to strike and kill.

But as I stand now,
a dying, unarmed soldier
could crush me
just lifting his boot.

Warriors possess strength
enough to level fortresses.
If I wish to lead troops,
I must command respect.
I cannot swish around
in the skirt of a peasant girl.

Knights wear heavy armor.
I must be able to shoulder
this weight and more.

But no one in Domrémy
owns a shield,
let alone a suit of armor.
Farmers carry pitchforks
and muck about in ratty boots.

I kick at the dirt,
trip on a jagged rock,
and skin my knee.
I cannot even walk without injury.
How will I face arrows and swords?

I pick up the cruel stone,
look to hurl it far into the field
for causing me pain.

But before I throw it away in anger,
the voice says:
You do not need a suit of armor
to master bearing the weight of a knight.

This is true.
I turn over the rock in my hand.
What if I discreetly tie stones
under my dress—
begin with two
and add more each day
until I wear the weight
of a young boy?

I smile and pick up
an armful of rocks.

ACHES AND PAINS

I know I live a life
of comfort and luxury
compared to most villagers in Domrémy—
but tying twenty-five stones
under apron and skirt,
or stuffed into my sleeves
such that they don't cut me
and no one detects them
when I bend to plow, wash,
or slop the pigs is *not* easy.
No knight would wear armor
this cumbersome, not one!
I long for a creaky metal suit.

I sweep the barn
and bend over
with a great sigh of pain
as if I am an old midwife,

when it occurs to me
that knights also ride horses into battle.

If I desire to ride rigorously,
wear armor, and brandish a weapon,
must I not straddle a horse like a man?
But La Pucelle,
the Virgin Maid,
cannot hitch up her skirt
and expect to be seen
as virtuous.

The last stall to be mucked
reeks of fresh manure.
In my haste to clean it quickly,
I slip on a patch of wet straw
and *merde* splatters my skirt.

Alone among the animals
I tear off my dress,
douse the stain with water and tallow,
smooth my knickers,
and hide as best as I can from view.
From a distance,
in my britches with my hair pulled back,
I might almost be mistaken for a boy,
instead of an indecent girl.
I stand so tall and lean
and without womanly curves.

I slip back into my gown
laden with rocks
and sulk.

I was born
to be a warrior,
not a princess,
yet I remain
confined
by a stupid dress.

CATHERINE THE WIFE

My sister and the blacksmith's son
were betrothed when they were ten.
Catherine and Mother have nestled away
bowls, blankets, baskets,
since she was a young girl
to help my sister create
her own home.

This afternoon Catherine and Marc
will stand together under a veil
and accept our priest's blessing.
They'll break a ceremonial coin in two,
and each retain a half
as a symbol of their union.

Father must give Marc's family
five sheep, a bushel of grain,
and a pig as my sister's dowry.
And Marc's father will provide
thirteen silver coins

as the bride-price.
It took several years
to negotiate this,
for Father to barter away
his eldest daughter
in much the same fashion
as he trades cattle.

Catherine has always been pretty,
but today she looks like sunlight
shimmering on the lake.
Dressed in her blue wedding gown,
she seems far more than
two years my elder.

Mother swipes away several tears
as she brushes Catherine's hair
and ties a ribbon around her wrist.

I stand in the corner
and try to act
like my mouth's not dry
and I slept well last night,
when, in fact,
I slept not at all.

I will be the only daughter now.
As much as I used to resent
standing in perfect Catherine's wake,

I have lately grown to appreciate
the freedom of being second,
the daughter my parents
will deal with at some later point.
Now I take Catherine's place.

How will Mother and I
do all the laundry, tend the garden,
and cook every meal
without my sister's aid?

I want to beg Catherine to stay,
to delay leaving home,
to remain here,
to help distract everyone
from my comings and goings,
to be my unwitting ally
and great support.

I have training to complete,
God's work to do.
How will I be La Pucelle
and my parents' only daughter?

LEARNING TO RIDE

We raise sheep, cattle, pigs,
have chickens, an ox,
two dogs, and a cat.
But we do not own a horse.

Knights grow up with saddles and steeds,
grip reins almost
as soon as they can walk.

Only one family in the village
has a horse,
but they are rumored to be
of Burgundian blood.
Father would surely whip me
like a bowl of cream
if I set a boot on their property.
So it is imperative that I not get caught.

With less than an hour
before my family will note my absence,
I loiter at the edge of Monsieur Le Mans's property.

The farmstead is as desolate
as an overcast sky.
Their mare grazes
alone in the pasture.
Her brown coat gleams
like she's been dipped in bronze.

I hook my legs over the fence
and extend a handful of carrots.
"Here, girl, I won't hurt you."

The horse approaches me slowly,
trying to judge whether I mean her harm.
She glares at me with suspicious eyes,
then halts ten feet away.
I toss her the carrots,
but she refuses to touch them
until I hop down from the fence
and back away.

After a week of my tossing her carrots,
the horse trusts me enough
to eat from my hand.
She even allows me to stroke her neck.

The day the mare nuzzles my chin,
I draw up enough courage
to climb the fence,
hitch up my skirt,
and sling my legs around her back.
She jostles and rears
as if attacked by angry hornets,
and I nearly plummet to the ground.
But she soon returns to calmness,
and with gentle prodding,
she trots me along the fence.

Three days later, when I approach
with my hair tucked up under my garden hat,
wearing a pair of Pierre's trousers
that I stole from the mending basket,
the horse fails to recognize me.

After long sniffing of my hand and neck,
she realizes who I am
and allows me to mount
and straddle her.

The difference between
riding in trousers
and riding in a skirt
is like boating across the lake
instead of swimming.
Outfitted like a man,

I can steady myself
to the rhythm
of her movement.

As we pick up speed,
I spot Monsieur Le Mans
heading toward me with a pitchfork.

"Get off my horse, boy!"
he yells.

I dismount and run
as fast as my legs will permit
across meadow and stream,
never once looking back,
until I stand well within
the safety of the woods.

Only then does it strike me:
Monsieur believed I was a boy.

The next day the mare
is not out to pasture,
nor the next,
nor the day after that.

My riding lessons
swiftly
end.

SWORDSMAN

Because I can no longer develop
equestrian skills,
I teach myself to handle a sword.

I slice through the air
with my family's ax.
But whacking at a tree trunk
lacks the nuances of a swordfight.
In less than ten minutes
wielding an ax grows more exasperating
than a day pulling the plow.

So I bind a kitchen knife
to a stick, then fasten a twig
crosswise to create a handle,
and my sword is born.

Far in the fields
I slay withering stalks.
As if they are a row of soldiers
I whirl and surprise
them with my steel.

But crops and men of hay
do not scream or bleed or die.

I cannot imagine harming
an actual soldier.
Murder is the gravest of sins.
I hope I am never
forced to kill.

WHO AM I?

Soon I must convince others
that I am La Pucelle.

But just because I do not wish
to be someone's wife
does not mean I hoped to be
a soldier.

I feel as awkward
as a three-legged horse
around the boys of my village.
How will I survive in an army of men?

People believed me odd before;
imagine what they will think
when they see me
brandish a sword and shield.

And if I am La Pucelle,
what becomes of
Jehanne of Domrémy,
the daughter, the sister, the girl?

Is she swallowed
like the sun
into the vast darkness of night?

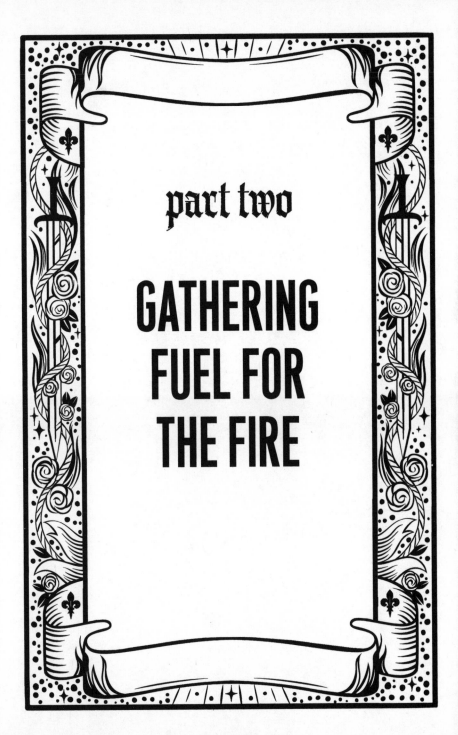

part two

GATHERING FUEL FOR THE FIRE

A FIRST ATTEMPT

Spring 1428

Sixteen now,
I can no longer play at soldier.

If I am to help save France,
I need an army.

God instructs me to ask
Sir Robert de Baudricourt for one.
He's a captain of the dauphin Charles,
who heaven decrees with my aid
will be crowned king of France.

Captain Baudricourt
dwells in Vaucouleurs,
ten miles from our village,
ten miles farther than I dare
venture on my own.

For years,
I have pretended

that I have no purpose
beyond crops and prayers.
But today a gate opens.

Uncle Laxart visits.
Along with his sacks of grain
I ride back in Uncle's cart
to Burey, a hamlet
on the edge of Vaucouleurs.

●◆●

Safe in Burey and without fear
that my immediate family
will try to hinder or silence me.
My uncle is the first person
I tell about my mission.
When I ask him to introduce me
to Sir Robert Baudricourt,
he pounds the table.
"I will not take you to see him. *Non!*
Tu es complètement folle, Jehanne!"

"Please, Uncle.
God has chosen me
to save France,
and I need your help.
If not by God's will,

I should have no desire
to enter battle."

I argue until my uncle
looks as if he has traveled
three days in a blinding storm
and wonders whether
I am sent by God
or the devil himself.
He covers his ears,
as if the sound of my voice
drives him mad.
His eyelids droop
with exhaustion.
Uncle shakes his head and sighs.

Finally, he agrees.

●◆●

Uncle Laxart removes
his cap, bows his head,
and introduces me to Sir Robert.

Before my uncle can
replace his woolen hat,
I step forward and announce
to Captain Baudricourt,

"The King of Heaven
demands that you supply me
an army so that
I can liberate France."

Sir Robert's laughter sounds
like a murder of crows
nesting in his throat.
"This is the daughter of Jacques d'Arc?
Why, she's mad!
Give her a good slapping, Laxart,
and return her to her father!"

My uncle grabs me by the elbow,
but I turn back to Sir Robert,
not a waver to my words.
"I am La Pucelle, the Maid!
I am sent by God
to crown the dauphin king
and to save France.
And you will
deliver me an army, sir!"

Captain Baudricourt's slanted eyes
weigh whether I'm insulting or amusing.
He smiles. "I might deliver *you*
to the army, girl, and see how long
La Pucelle remains a virgin there."

Everyone in the room
rocks with laughter,
but I am not shaken.

I open my mouth to respond.
But before I can,
Uncle Laxart yanks me
out of the room.

He raises no hand to me.
Still, my uncle's words sting like a whip.
"Jehanne, you foolish girl!
You have humiliated us all."

I remain silent as the stars
during the long ride home.
It is not my intention
to bring shame to my family,
only to follow God's command.
But perhaps my speech was too bold.
Perhaps my tongue
should have been coated with honey,
not brine.
If it would spare my family embarrassment,
I might alter the timbre of my voice,
but I will never abandon
my mission
or my words.

CATHERINE'S GOOD NEWS

As returning birds chirp
the beginning of spring,
my sister announces
that a baby grows within her.

Since she married
she has twice been pregnant,
but before she felt either baby kick
the little one was lost.
This time Catherine
rounds like a pumpkin.
Mother feels confident
this child will survive.

I never thought my father
cared much for infants,
but he struts around,
heralds this news
as if he won a prize
for raising the largest pig.

He clearly glories in the idea
of becoming a grandfather.

At least one of his daughters
acts respectably,
understands her place and duty.

And then there is me.

SECOND RETREAT TO NEUFCHÂTEAU
July 1428

No one in my family
speaks of my visit to Vaucouleurs,
though all know what happened.

Mother becomes
more silent than steam.

Like owls lurking in the night,
my brothers monitor my every step.

My father fumes
as if I poison his house
with the malodor
of a feral cat in heat.
I am marked with the scent
of impertinence and disobedience.
I have dishonored him.

The implicit threat of punishment
dangles around my neck.

I had best not attempt
another ploy like Vaucouleurs.

•◆•

We learn that once again
Burgundian soldiers
approach our village.
Toothless, bedraggled,
and slathered in grime,
this band of marauders
smells worse than rotten fish.

My family packs up
our most valuable possessions
and heads south, as before,
to the safety of Neufchâteau.

We lodge at the inn of
the widow Madame la Rousse.
I help our hostess in the kitchen,
where I hear many stories
from French soldiers
who visit the inn—
how they stormed fortresses,
fought sword to sword against the enemy,
and waged a night attack
to free prisoners from English cells.
It's a great joy to meet men-at-arms

I admire, but I'm careful
never to be alone around the soldiers,
for I understand that I must remain,
without question, the Virgin Maid,
for La Pucelle means just that.
My virtue is more precious to me
than a thousand gold coins.

Madame la Rousse
speaks a more proper French
than one hears in Domrémy.
I practice the lilt of her *l*,
the roll of her *r*
and learn not to run my words together
like unblotted ink.

But after a month at the inn,
Father announces
that we cannot hide
from the conflict forever,
and we return to Domrémy.

●◆●

The Burgundian soldiers
left behind their stench
and little else.

They torched everything,
burned down the Saint-Rémy church,
a consecrated house,
as if it were nothing more
than a toolshed.

As I rummage through
the charred remnants of my town,
I know something must be done,
and soon.

A MARRIAGE FOR JEHANNE

Father must have hustled about
Neufchâteau busier than a squirrel.
As a consequence of my behavior
in Vaucouleurs,
he arranged a marriage for me
without my consent
to a man I have never met,
a farmer's son from Burey.

Father does not understand
that I cannot marry,
for it is against God's will,
and my own.
He refuses to hear about
or accept my mission.

Few girls possess the courage
to stand up to their fathers,
and yet like a soldier

facing her first battle,
I summon the nerve.

To stop my marriage
from occurring
and annul the betrothal,
I must travel to Toul,
the county seat.
I walk fifteen miles
alone as a ship lost at sea
and plead my case in court.

I implore the judge,
"I never pledged to marry
any boy. I should not be forced
into matrimony.
My virtue must remain
unsullied and indisputable."

The judge scratches his head,
as if I am a greater puzzlement
than snowflakes in August.
"You are not property, Jehanne,
so if you did not enter
into the engagement
of your own free will,
you need not marry this man."

I lift my chin and smile.
"I agreed to nothing."

I win my case,
but I set myself at further odds
with my father.
Sickened by the sight of me,
whenever I enter the house
or barn or field,
he exits.

I fear it is time for me
to leave home
and never return.

OH, BROTHERS

Jean frustrated me before,
snoring under his hat
while Pierre and I toiled
until our arms ached,
but now my brother forgoes his nap
to drive and direct me
like I am the mule
who pulls our plow.
Jean gazes at the sun
and comments that
it is nearly midday
and I have not
swept out the stalls,
nor begun gathering kindling,
chopping firewood,
or tending Mother's herbs.

When I open my mouth to protest,
Pierre, who used to side with me
against Jean's autocracy,

holds his finger to his lips,
then balls his fist.
I spoke in court.
I spoke to Sir Robert.
I would be wise to say
nothing now.

I close my eyes
and pray for strength.

THE SIEGE OF ORLÉANS
October 1428

When we learn that the English
surround the city of Orléans,
my village buzzes
with as much fear and fury
as birds fluttering
inside a chimney.

On the Loire River
at the intersection
of several major trade routes,
the walled city
stands as France's last bastion
against the enemy.
Orléans is the heart
inside my country's chest.
We cannot survive
without it.

Hungry wolves lurking
outside the wall,
our enemies
want to overtake Orléans
more than anywhere else.

English troops built bastilles,
towers that house their weapons and men,
at the city's gates
to prevent French reinforcements,
food, and supplies
from entering the city.

We are told
that the citizens of Orléans despair.
It is rumored
that the frightened dauphin
plans to exile himself
to a foreign country,
to desert the southern capital of Chinon,
to desert France entirely.

No one knows what to do—

Except me.

CHILDBIRTH

A sorrow greater
than I have ever known
rivers through my veins.
Last night my sister
lost her baby,
then her life.

How can Catherine
be gone from us
faster than the break of day?

At night
below the chirp of crickets,
muffled sobs
echo through the house.

Mother wails and weeps,
has little use for her bed.
She circles the kitchen,

constantly searching
for something she cannot find.

Jean forfeits all desire to order
Pierre and me around.
He works tirelessly in the fields,
then prays beside me in church.

Pierre drifts away,
quiet and often alone.
He retreats to the stables,
to the cows,
his energy vanquished.

Surely God has a reason
for calling Catherine and her baby
to his side.
But even with that consolation,
my family aches as though our bones
have been crushed under a mountain.

Last year when my feet
stretched beyond my shoes,
Catherine gifted me her new boots,
boots she scrimped and saved to buy.
She smiled and said how lucky she was
that her old ones still fit.

I wish that the first person
I shared my mission with,
my calling from God,
had been my sister.
Catherine would have believed
and supported me.
She always did.

Now I truly am
my parents' only daughter.
And a grave disappointment
at that.

But perhaps
it will change.

BACK TO BAUDRICOURT
December 1428

The air has altered
since I last came to Vaucouleurs.
It carries a scent
desperate as a graveyard.
People hunger for hope.
When winds blow around
tales of a young maid
who is sent by God
to save France,
many feel as if sun breaks
through the gloom.

I am welcomed by
the well-respected Le Royers
to stay at their home inside the city.
A crowd gathers outside the door
to gawk at the Maid
from the old prophecy, La Pucelle.
In my homespun russet-red dress,
they wonder: How can I,

a slim sixteen-year-old girl,
be France's savior?
And yet they long to believe.
We all need to believe
in something right now,
myself included.

A knight in the city garrison,
Jean de Metz, taunts me,
"What are you doing here, girl?
Is it not fated that the dauphin
shall be driven from his kingdom,
and we shall all turn English?"

Even though he is ten years
my senior, I stare the man down.
"Before mid-Lent
I must be with the king,
even if I must wear my legs
down to the knees.
God has ordained
the salvation of France,
and for this purpose
I was born."

Jean de Metz stares hazily at me,
as though he has been struck
with a steel rod by my words.
I expect him to mock

or question me further,
because so far
all I have met with
is resistance and rejection,
but he does not.
Instead it is as though he too
follows a divine order.
The good knight kneels
in chivalry
and pledges allegiance
to me and my cause.
Jean miraculously
accepts and believes
that all I say and do
is willed by God.

And astoundingly, he is not
the only soldier to follow me.
Another nobleman and knight,
Bertrand de Poulengy,
also vows to support La Pucelle.

Perhaps with these knights beside me,
I no longer need Sir Robert
to reach the dauphin.
Perhaps our small band
can go it alone.

IMPATIENCE IS NOT A VIRTUE

The next day
I lead a small party of supporters
nearly one-fourth the distance
I must travel to Chinon
to see the dauphin.

But then I turn my company around.

I cannot be led by impatience.
God assured me
that Captain Baudricourt
will give me an audience
and what I require
if I endure
like the snow iris
and hibernate through winter's end,
rather than burst prematurely
from the soil.

In truth, I need
Sir Robert's personal introduction
if I wish to meet the dauphin.
Otherwise I may never
be admitted to court.

WAITING TO BLOOM

For nearly a month
I wait at the Le Royers' home
while Sir Robert fiddles his thumbs,
unsure what to do with me.

He sends a priest
to exorcise any demons
I might possess.
The priest douses me with holy water
and cries, *"Vade retro me satana!"*
Were I harboring evil,
I would convulse
and fall to the ground
as devilish spirits left my body.

But I stand, unmoved,
and smile. I ask the father,
"Now that is done,
might you hear my confession?"

The priest agrees.
We pray the *Paternoster* together,
and *le prêtre* reports back
to Sir Robert
that my motives appear pure
and that my calling seems divine.

But still Baudricourt remains as frozen
as the February ground.

So I continue to wait,
patient as *la fleur*.
I use the delay
to train with the local garrison.

My time with Monsieur Le Mans's mare
prepared me better than I expected.
I shock myself and more importantly
Jean de Metz and his fellow knights
when I ride a destrier, a warhorse,
with immediate ease.
They marvel at how
I wield a lance and shield
as if I have been conditioning
to be a soldier all my life.

As the town watches
a small girl from Domrémy
transform into a soldier,
more and more people believe
that I am La Pucelle.

LIKE MY ELDEST BROTHER

Jean de Metz arrives each morning
to accompany me to the arena
where we ride and train.
He scouts the road ahead
as if he searches out sinkholes,
then clears away rats, debris—
anything or anyone
who might cause me harm.
He reminds me of Jacquemin,
my protective brother, always suspicious
that danger may lie ahead.

The difference
is that Jean de Metz
treats me more like
a younger brother
instead of a little sister.
He arms me with a sword,
then lunges full speed
at my chest.

My shield blocks his steel,
but this just encourages
Jean de Metz to strike again
with greater force.
He trusts that in battle
I will fight as does
any knight,
that in the arena
I can protect myself.
Even though I wear a dress,
he never acts like
I am a girl.

THOUGHTS OF HOME

I am told Father
no longer allows my name
to be uttered in his presence,
that he wishes to wash away
all memory of me
as one desires to rid oneself
of the taste of turned milk.

Likewise, when visions
of my father's farm
sneak into my dreams,
I light them on fire,
try to sear them from my brain.

I cannot be held back
by what I used to be.
And after the loss of Catherine,
the happiness and security
of my home shattered
like an egg upon the ground,

the shell fractured,
the insides seeping
into dirt and grave.

I am grateful
to look forward,
to follow God's mission,
to have purpose,
not to swim in sorrow,
not to drown in a lake
of loss.

THE BROTHERHOOD OF KNIGHTS

Jean de Metz sharpens his sword
as he explains that
he has a family outside
the one into which he was born.
All good knights do.

For he has brothers
not bound by name or place
who will lay down
their lives to save his own.
Brothers who share something deeper
than the blood coursing
through their veins,
for they have shed blood together.

He tells me
I will be a part
of this family.

My eyes glaze with tears
as I brush off my skirt.
I wonder if that
will truly be.

NO MORE DRESS

Is it proper to visit the king
in the same dress
one wears to slop pigs?

The citizens of Vaucouleurs
think not.
They want me to resemble the army
I will lead.
So no more dress.
They gift me tailor-made
men's clothes of the finest fabrics
I have ever worn,
for it will be safer if I travel
the three hundred fifty miles
through enemy territory
in the costume of a man.
I crop my hair
to complete my disguise.

Even though his people
support me, only the hand of God
stirs Baudricourt from his torpor.

What finally persuades
Sir Robert to grant me
six of his men, a formal letter
of introduction to the king,
and a black steed for my journey,
some consider a miracle.

I inform Sir Robert,
on the very day it occurs,
and far before any news of the battle
could reach Vaucouleurs,
that the French
suffer a great loss
outside Orléans, near Rouvray.

When a courier confirms
my premonition,
Sir Robert nearly falls off his chair.

I implore him on bended knee,
"Please, I must be away
before it is too late!"

Sir Robert has no choice
except to grant my request.
He rolls his eyes
and waves me off with the words
"Go, and come what may."

THE JOURNEY TO CHINON
February 1429

We move
through the night
like bandits,
waiting until dusk
before venturing
beyond the gates of Vaucouleurs.

Chinon lies a world away,
three hundred fifty miles to the west,
a rigorous ride
through Burgundian territory.
But God promises our safety.
He decrees:
**You and your party shall
reach Chinon in eleven days.**

To do this I must
cast my gaze
like a beast with three eyes:

one eye ahead and one behind,
and a third focused on my own men.

Sent by Baudricourt to accompany me
are the two noble knights
Jean de Metz and Bertrand Poulengy;
a servant of Poulengy, Julien;
a messenger for the dauphin and royal family
called Colet de Vienne; Richard the Archer;
and Jean de Honecourt, who serves
both Colet and Richard.

But only the good knights
champion my cause.
The four other men
refuse to believe
that I am sent by God
and do not enjoy being bridled
to a peasant girl.

I overhear these men plot
to strip me of my purity
like a pack of feral hounds.

On the second night
they ambush me,
muffle my screams of protest,
and hold me down
to do their dirty deed.

Overpowered
and helpless as a snared rabbit,
I tremble in terror.
But to the men's great shock,
they can feel no lust for me.
All four soldiers
fall soft with impotence.

Baudricourt's men
lace tight their trousers,
convinced immediately
that I must be heavenly sent,
for what else could have prevented them
from ravaging me?
From this point forward
all six of my escorts pledge
undying devotion.

Unified in our mission,
we race through the countryside.
Only when dawn
wrestles free from darkness
do we halt to sleep.

Though our party travels
under the cover of night,
we might still attract attention.
So we avoid all roads
and wade through forest and glen.

No enemy, no raider,
no river or storm
ever impedes our progress.

I pray many times each day.
But without a church in which
to confess and hear mass,
I feel as if an arrow pierces my heart.

A day's ride from Chinon,
my tension uncoils.
Even though we are still
inside enemy territory,
we attend a mass in Auxerre.
I pray so intensely
that tears flood my face
like a river swelling its banks.

I alone understand
that the siege *must* be lifted
from Orléans forthwith.

I have scarce little time
to see the dauphin crowned.
For as I kneel before His altar,
God tells me:
Before you reach twenty years,
you will die.

part three

KINDLING

TAKE ME TO THE DAUPHIN

I cannot think about my fate,
but only move forward.
A bird in flight,
I never stop flapping my wings,
never look down,
and thereby forget my impending fall.

I send a letter to the dauphin
requesting an audience with him
and wait in Sainte-Catherine-de-Fierbois
like a faithful child.
I go to mass
as often as the priests do
and pray on tireless knees
in Saint Catherine's shrine.

My entrance into the city of Chinon
requires the dauphin's permission.
Until Charles bids me come,

I remain barred from the castle
as if I am an enemy.

Banging swords clamor
over what should be done with me.
Some want to welcome me at once.
Other advisers whisper
into Charles's ear
that I do the devil's bidding.

But the dauphin,
whom I must help crown
the next king of France,
will see me for who I am.

DEAD MAN'S SHOES

Two long days pass
before I am invited to court.

Chinon's castle sits above the city,
an eagle's nest perched so high
it appears to scrape the clouds.
White stone turrets strung
with the dauphin's coat of arms
stand like guards.

Flanked with the support
of my two knights,
I ride toward the castle.
A priest, Jean Pasquerel,
joins our retinue.
He offers me
daily confession and counsel.
I am beyond grateful for his company.

As we mount the stairs
leading to the king's quarters,
a soldier roughly cries out,
"Is that not the Maid there?
I swear to God
if I had her for a night
she would be a virgin no more!"

Hot tears brim my eyes.
Why are so many men
insistent on stripping me
of my purity?
Are they so threatened
by a girl with an ounce of freedom
and control?

I holler back to the man,
"Why do you take
the name of the Lord in vain
when you are so close
to your own death?
Do you not wish to see heaven?"

The soldier holds his belly
as laughter rumbles through him.

An hour later, however,
the man stops laughing,
stops breathing.

He falls into the moat
and drowns,
as I predicted he would.

A SHORT PRAYER

Before we enter
the dauphin's chamber,
I fall to my knees.
Here begins my real task.

I am seventeen,
a small girl wearing boy's clothes
entering a room of royalty.

Inside, I tremble like a child
abandoned in the wilderness.
I hear a bear growling
in the darkness
but know not where
it hides.

Please, God,
grant me the strength
to never wander from my path,

to accomplish my goals,
and to conceal my fears.

MEETING THE DAUPHIN
March 1429

I traipse past
the splendor of royalty—
heads adorned with tall conical hennins,
bejeweled necks, arms, and hands,
garments more fetching than peacock feathers.

The court regards
my dusty black doublet,
coarse tunic, and short black hair
as though I reek of manure.
Yet these are the finest clothes
I have ever worn.

Undaunted,
I seek the dauphin.
I have a message for him
and no other.

But the dauphin's councillors
aim to trick me,
want me to stumble in my boots
and be shown as a fraud.
For although I have never seen
the son who will be king,
I know that the man
who wears the royal crest,
introduces himself as Charles,
and bids me kiss his ring
is *not* the dauphin.

I spin around until I spot,
dressed in the clothes
of a lesser courtier,
the dauphin crouching in a corner
of the chamber.

I kiss Charles's feet and exclaim,
"Most noble Lord Dauphin,
I have come and am sent by God
to help you and your kingdom."

A SIGN

The dauphin recoils from me,
sharp as a whip.
Even though I plucked
him like a needle
among the hay,
he does not believe
that I am heaven-sent.
Somehow, I must earn
his confidence.

I mute the tumult around us.
Charles alone matters.
"Please, gentle Dauphin,
let us retire to a private chamber,
and I will prove to you
that I am sent by God."

But Charles does not shift.
Only after his mother-in-law,

Yolande of Aragon,
whispers into his ear
does Charles motion
for me to follow him.

I close the chapel door
and gaze up
at the beautiful golden altar
where my dauphin must pray daily.
I have heard that the dauphin
is almost as pious as I am.
I motion for Charles
to kneel with me
and pray that God
will provide him a sign
so the dauphin will know
that I speak the truth.

He falls reverently
to his knees before the cross,
closes his eyes,
and recites the *Paternoster*.

I whisper,
"Dearest Dauphin,
you prayed that
if you are indeed the heir
to the kingdom of France,

God would protect you.
I am sent to assure you
that you will be crowned king."

Charles remains
fixated on the altar.

"Sweet Dauphin,
I was born a lowly peasant girl.
I would never leave my home
to take up arms
solely by my own volition."

Charles looks me
squarely in the eyes
for the first time.
"I did pray for God's
guidance and protection,
but anyone might have
guessed that.
I am not yet convinced you are
who you say you are."

I clasp my hands
and look to heaven.
What can I say
to make him believe me?
Miraculously, these words
escape my lips:

"I know, Royal Dauphin,
that you humbly asked our Lord
to help you escape
to the court of either
Spain or Scotland."

Charles's cheeks turn
a shade of red deeper
than his bulbous nose.
"How could you know that?"

"Sire, I am sent by God."

Charles bows his head
toward the altar
as a great light fills the room
and a sign appears.
"Is that a golden crown?"
he asks, more awestruck
than a man standing
before the gates of heaven.

"Yes, and it belongs upon
my dauphin's head."

Charles clasps my hands.
"I believe it is true.
You are La Pucelle
sent by God."

CONVICTION

I am a girl who has never
seen war, who has never
witnessed one man kill another.
I march forward and speak
with the surety of a queen,
but what if I reach the battlefield
and freeze at the horror
of blood and loss?
What if even with God's aid
my humanness, my femininity,
somehow defeat me?

Are there not moments
in the middle of the night
when I wonder
if I really can lift
the siege from Orléans?

If I fail to deliver
all that I promise,

I let down my family,
my country, my king,
myself, and God.

I will be exiled.
I will have no home,
not on earth or in heaven.
I will belong nowhere,
to no one.

That cannot be God's will,
and it certainly is not mine.
I must be the girl who saves France.

MY EXAMINATION
March 1429

Although Charles believes in me,
his advisers remain wary
as a drizzling rain.
They convince the dauphin
that I should be tested
by men of the church
to make sure I am not
a child of the devil.

I have faced questioning before
in Vaucouleurs.
I convinced the dauphin
of my mission.
God tells me
I should fear nothing
but delay.

We travel to Poitiers,
the home of Parliament
in Armagnac France.

My first test:
I am examined by la dauphine,
Charles's wife, and her ladies
to see if my maidenhood is intact.
This is not a comfortable test,
being poked and prodded
in the most private of areas.
But despite riding a warhorse
across rivers and valleys,
I am found to be
a clear and true virgin
without corruption or violation.

My second test:
Eighteen clerics
interrogate me
and probe my soul,
as if they wish to trap me
with a cage of words.

"Do you believe in God?"
one man asks.

"Yes, more than you do,"
I answer.

Laughter bursts
from the flock of priests.

I explain that I have been sent
by the King of Heaven
for two reasons:
to lift the siege on Orléans
and to lead the king to Reims
for his anointing and coronation.

Eyebrows rise and lips smirk,
as if the clerics taste something sour.

"What language
does your voice speak?"
a cleric from Languedoc
who speaks in a rural dialect
asks me.

"A better tongue than you do,"
I tell him with a smile.

The holy men snicker,
amused by my quick wit.
Still their skepticism remains,
thicker than clay.
The clerics assert that if God wishes
to deliver the people of France
from their present calamities,
He could do so without my aid.
The dauphin need not give soldiers
to a girl.

But God does not fight earthly battles.
Soldiers do.
What God does is decide
who wins the war.

The clerics pore over their papers
as if the parchment will speak aloud.

They finally retort
that God cannot wish them
to believe in me
unless he sends them a sign.
They refuse to advise the dauphin
to entrust me with soldiers
merely on my bare assertions.

I stare at the eighteen holy men
encircling me
and inhale slowly.
Then, with quiet passion, I repeat,
"Lead me to Orléans,
and I will show you
the signs I was sent to make."

The room erupts into argument
as if a cannon just exploded
before the council.
The head examiner
bangs on his table,

demanding silence.

"We shall debate this further
without her who calls herself La Pucelle,
then present our assessment
to the dauphin."

BROTHERLY ADVICE

Jean de Metz has traversed
the graveyard of many a battlefield.
Still he laughs and jokes
as if the world is full of good humor.
I ask him how he can be
lighthearted and patient
when we have so much to accomplish
and yet are denied boats,
forbidden to swim,
and forced to tread water.
We must endlessly wait
for others to understand our mission
and then provide us
with what God knows
we need and should have—
an army.

Jean de Metz smiles.
"Faith is largely patience,
is it not, La Pucelle?"

I reluctantly nod my head.

But if that is true,
why do I lose my patience,
yet never lose my faith?

FITTING IN

I refuse to do nothing
but pray and wait.

When the soldiers in Poitiers
welcome me into their field,
intrigued noblemen gather
to watch me train.
Like gawking crows,
their jaws drop
when they see
that my skills rival
those of the knights around me.

For the first time
I do not wonder
how I fit in,
I just do.

I belong among
these men-at-arms
like water belongs
in the sea.

THE DUKE OF ALENÇON

Today a duke
who bows, as I do,
to the dauphin
enters my training arena.
He eyes me as if
wings sprout
from my shoulder blades.

A growl hides
under my tongue.
I do not wish
to defend myself
to this nobleman.
I do not wish
to defend myself to anyone
today.

On a borrowed destrier
I charge across the track,
kick up rain clouds of dust.

Not to boast,
but with little practice,
I ride as expertly as the king's guard.
Without instruction,
except from above,
I heave a lance
under one arm and charge,
fearless as a bull,
my horns set to attack.

When my steed halts
before him,
the Duke of Alençon laughs.

I slant my eyes.
"Why, sir, do you mock me?"

He removes his helmet,
props it on one hip.
"Are you La Pucelle,
the maid about whom
tales are being woven
faster than thread
spools on a wheel?"

I step toward him.
"I am she."

Our eyes lock
like two swords clashing.

The duke holds my gaze.
He neither retreats nor escalates.
He looks at me as I have
never been regarded before,
as if we are of equal stature—
not a peasant beside royalty,
not a woman and a man.
He nods.
"Yes, I believe you are."

AN ALLY

The duke cannot be
more than five years
my senior.
Tall in stature
with a ready smile,
a wit as nimble as his sword,
and pockets ever lined
with coins for the poor—
I believe him to be
the perfect knight.

I never expected anyone
of his position
to truly champion my cause.
But this duke teaches me
to charm nobility
as well as dismantle our enemy
with eyes more fearsome
than a dragon.

He extends a hand
of friendship,
and I grasp it tightly.

If the Duke of Alençon,
who is a cousin of the dauphin Charles,
can be persuaded
to stand by my side,
perhaps there is hope
that others of title and command
will follow me too.

INTRODUCTIONS

I may think highly
of the Duke of Alençon,
but will the first knight,
Jean de Metz,
who stood by my side
before anyone else dared,
agree?

My three brothers
often acted like goats,
clashing horns, butting heads,
to establish who would claim
the top of the hill.
I fear rivalry and bravado
may enter the brotherhood
of knights as well.

I invite both men to dinner,
expecting I will need to
smooth awkward silences

and disentangle challenging words.
But I am as wrong
as a flying frog.

"I fought beside your father
at Agincourt. He was a great
warrior and commander."
Jean de Metz bows his head.

"And your reputation
precedes you, Jean."

Compliments shoot across the table
like arrows striking bull's-eyes.
Wine, laughter, and memories
flow heartily between the men.

If anyone teeters on the fringe
of the conversation,
it is me.
And I could not be
more pleased.

BECAUSE I WEAR ARMOR

The Duke of Alençon
gives me a white destrier,
far grander than the one
Sir Robert provided.

But there is no greater gift
he can offer
than what he has already granted me—
his camaraderie.

Yet if I were not La Pucelle,
just Jehanne of Domrémy,
the duke and I
would never be in company.
I understand who I am now
riding a horse,
instead of leading it to pasture.
I am a soldier,
no longer a girl,
never to be a woman.

God has told me
my life will be short.
I will have no future time
for love or family.

Today
my heart seems to drown
in a never-ending storm
over this.
A part of me
feels as empty
as a bucket with a hole.

NEVER SHOW MY FEAR

Though storms may roil
through my stomach
and my pulse speed
faster than a blustering wind,
though my palms may sweat
as does sweltering August
and my legs tremble
like a fawn first learning to walk,
I must bundle my fears inside.

Because I am a girl,
it is even more important
that no one catch
a glimmer of doubt in my eyes,
nor see a hint of fright
cross my brow.
I can only reveal my trepidations
in solitude and prayer.

PRAY

A crowd cheers
as I walk toward the cathedral.
The peasants rejoice in knowing
the King of Heaven can raise up
the smallest among us.

As I pray at the altar,
Father Pasquerel kneels beside me
and says, "It was the prophet Isaiah
who foretold that the smallest one
will become a thousand,
and the least create a mighty nation."

The French people believe that I,
La Pucelle of the old prophecy,
who is sent by God,
will do just that,
restore our mighty nation.
They brick a fortress

of love and support around me
that fortifies
my will and my heart.

WHAT THEY DETERMINE

Perhaps the council
has seen that the French people
follow me into the cathedral,
embrace more pious beliefs,
and praise God, as I do,
in every moment.

Perhaps the priests see
how the people adore the Maid
and need to believe in her.
Like starving troops
who have long lacked nourishment,
the people now find their bellies
are satiated with hope.

Perhaps the robed men also witness
how the soldiers in Poitiers
accept me as one of their own.

The commission of clerics concludes
that no evil is to be found in me,
only goodness, humility,
virginity, devotion,
honesty, and simplicity.
They tell the dauphin
he should give me an army.

GATHERING TROOPS

April 6, 1429

Who will follow me?
The commoners have not
the weapons or skill
to take the battlefield.
It is the nobility
who must support me.

And thankfully, they do.
Noblemen arrive in Chinon
like bees swarming a hive.

Some of these men
join an army for the first time.
Steel fused by fire,
the loyal Frenchmen
band together
for a righteous cause.

The question then becomes whether
the other commanders

will trust a peasant girl to lead them.
Unfortunately, God
does not reveal the answer to me.
He just urges me to combat.

My small entourage rides to Tours,
five miles northeast of Chinon.
The king entrusts Jean de Metz
with his purse.
Jean pays well the dozen commanders
with whom I am supposed to wage war
in the hope that this will encourage them
to support me fully.

With the dauphin's blessing,
we are all eager to fight the English.

But first we require
a few more preparations.

LOOKING THE PART

This is not a question
of a doublet and tunic
versus a dress.
It is about
forging armor that fits me.

I have never been more excited
about what covers my body
than I am when I receive
my custom-made, silver-white,
gleaming suit of armor.
Beneath it I wear
a stuffed doublet
and chain mail to protect
the parts of my body
not encased in steel.
Although this gear
weighs nearly forty pounds,
I move in it
as if I wear only my skin.

I commission
a twelve-foot standard
out of white linen fringed in silk.
I then ask that two angels
flanking the world
be painted on the banner
and that it bear the words *Jhesus Maria*.
With the dauphin's permission,
royal fleurs-de-lis
are sewn into my standard.
They promise victory.

The banner is more beautiful
than a wedding gown
and more crucial
than a sword or shield.

Still, I must carry a sword.
The voice reveals to me
that I should send for one
that lies in the church
of Sainte-Catherine-de-Fierbois,
buried behind the altar.
The sword belonged
first to Charles Martel
and was used
over seven hundred years ago
to slay infidels
for the first king of the Franks.

When they recover the sword,
though it is heavily rusted
the tarnish rubs away
as if it were merely rainwater.
The blade is etched with five crosses
as I foretold it would be.
Some say it is a miracle
for me to find this sword.
But I see it only,
like everything else I do
and shall do,
as following the will of God.

THE IMPORTANCE OF A FRENCH VICTORY

In my seventeen years
the French have known nothing
but defeat in major battles.
Weary and broken
like a cart without wheels,
we have struggled
just to maneuver through the mud.

Burgundian and English leaders
conquered Normandy from west to east.
They seized the French capital of Paris
and forced the dauphin to flee
his rightful home
as if a fire raged at his heels.

The English kings declare themselves
kings of France, whether or not
they have been consecrated by God,
whether or not it is right or wrong.

Our enemy presses ever south
with the desire to rule
all of France.
Defeating Orléans
will insure they succeed.
But the city,
like a fortress of armor,
has held.

Lifting the siege
on Orléans may provide
but one small victory
in what has been a long
and brutal war,
but we need this win
as surely as a man
drowning in a sinkhole
requires a rope.
Another defeat would be
deadly,
whereas a victory
could turn the tides.
This burden presses on my heart
and haunts my sleep.

DREAM OF FIRE

Again, English torches
ignite our barn in Domrémy,
and I am trapped inside.

However, in last night's reverie
when I call for help
someone answers back,
yells for my assistance.
But I cannot see who it is,
and worse, I cannot help him or her.
Flames circle higher and higher,
like spires in a cathedral,
as someone cries out in pain.

It is more terrifying
than being alone.

Only when I wake
do I realize
that the voice

calling back to me
was none other
than my own.

MY CONFESSION

I clasp the hands
of Father Pasquerel
as I unburden my heart.
Nothing I say to him
can be revealed to another.
That is the blessing and purpose
of holy confession.

Before I go to war,
even though God has assured
me I will not die in Orléans,
I need to clear my soul
of all I do not easily admit.

I bow my head, cross myself,
and admit that I fear
I may be leading my country
to great destruction.

I confess that I am afraid
to enter battle,
that I fear the sight
of men butchering men;
and I worry that
if I do not kill our enemy,
and I cannot kill anyone,
my soldiers will abandon me.

What if I reach the battlefield,
scream like a child,
and run away in fear?
What if I fall off my horse?

There are moments
I still fear that I am merely a girl,
and not La Pucelle,
that there is no La Pucelle,
and I may fail to do
what God asks of me.

I ask forgiveness
for my sins and doubts
and pray that with God's aid
I may persevere.

PREPARING FOR BATTLE

Outfitted for battle,
I move the twenty-five hundred men
who have amassed to fight beside me
to the town of Blois,
which lies halfway
between Tours and Orléans.

A large, boisterous commander La Hire,
whom the soldiers call the Hedgehog
because of his prickly
temperament, greets me.
"So, *you* are the Maid?"

He picks food out of his teeth
and spits it on the ground.
"My men and I are ready
to fight with you."

The camp is littered
with plunder and ungodliness.
Everywhere filth.
I try, but fail, to mask my horror.
His men are not ready to fight.

La Hire's laughter makes him cough.
"I see you have never lived
among men-at-arms, La Pucelle.
My men are as good as soldiers get.
The Goddoms[1] are the filthy shits.
But by our swords their foul blood
will soon be splattered on our tunics."

Father Pasquerel, who has accompanied me
since the day I first arrived in Chinon,
kisses La Hire on each cheek.
The Hedgehog flinches.
He prefers punches to kisses.
Father explains,
"The Maid wants your troops
to be confessed and free of sin."

---

[1] The Goddoms is a name the French called the English because they so often
heard English soldiers use the word "goddamn."

La Hire does not appear
to understand what the priest means.
It is as if the man
has never gone to church.

I explain with a smile,
"All who follow me into battle,
I must be assured
I will see again in heaven."

La Hire snorts.
"This is not the way
of most warriors,
but then you are not
an average soldier,
are you, Little Lady?"

I am the head commander,
not a little lady.
But I do not let his words
intimidate me.
I straighten my back.
"Try it
and see what victory comes."

The Hedgehog does not recoil
into a bristly ball or stick
his thorny needles in me.
He raises his eyebrows,

then yells with a voice
brusque enough to crack
apart the ground,
"Gather the men!
Damn if this won't be
an odd battle,
but I'll follow you
through heaven or hell
if it means that for once
the French shall be victors."

I cover my ears
to escape further profanity.
Perhaps the first confession
Father Pasquerel should hear
is Monsieur La Hire's.

part four

WHERE FIRST COMES SMOKE, NEXT COMES FIRE

A MESSAGE TO THE ENGLISH RULERS
April 25, 1429

We send the English a warning
as fierce as ten thousand arrows
launched into the air.
I doubt they will surrender.
Nevertheless, we offer them the chance.

I ask the English commanders
to surrender the keys of all the good towns
they have taken
and laid to waste in France.
For if they do not,
they should expect that La Pucelle
will shortly come upon them.
The English cannot withhold
the kingdom of France
from God.
King Charles will possess it.

I warn them not to bring themselves
to destruction
and demand that they answer me,
if they desire peace
in the city of Orléans.
If not, I promise
they and their men
will soon suffer great hurt.

THE ENGLISH REACTION

The enemy returns only
one of the two messengers
I dispatched with my letter.
I am told they laid tinder
beneath the stake
of the unlawfully held other
and are debating
whether to light it.

Further, the English captain Talbot
shows me no respect.
He delivers his reply to La Hire,
as if a woman can hold no authority.
Talbot writes to La Hire:
Tell the Armagnac whore
she'd best go home before
I catch her and burn her.

Once again, I am called names
aimed to rupture my spirit,
but today I let the insult
blow past me
like a puff of smoke.

I send my herald back to the enemy
bearing a new message:
Tell Talbot that
if he takes up arms,
we shall do likewise.
And let him burn me
if he can catch me.

THE ENEMY

As a child I imagined
an enemy was a fiend
with horns and gnarled teeth
hiding under my bed.
But now I understand
that an enemy
can look like a neighbor,
friend, or brother.
I ask Jean de Metz
how he lifts his sword
to strike down
another man
when he so resembles
the one fighting
beside him.

He tells me
the instinct to survive
runs even deeper in the soul
than does the conscience.

If an ax flies
toward your head,
you will lift your shield,
then, before taking a breath,
engage your sword
to remove all chance
of a secondly deadly blow.
Thought factors little
on the battlefield.
The body works
beyond the mind.

La Hire listens
to us prick-eared
as a rabbit.
He snorts, shakes his head,
and thunders that
what my friend the knight
fails to mention
is the thrill
that is battle.
La Hire says
I will know my enemy
by the loathing in his eye
and the rage of his tongue.
The high-and-mighty
English captain Talbot:
to knock him from his horse
will send a rush

through my veins
that nothing can equal.
To stand soldier to soldier
knowing one of you
will die
engages more than instinct;
you learn
what it truly means
to be alive.

WE ARE AN ARMY OF GOD

We leave for Orléans at dawn.
I feel assured
we will triumph
when we encounter
our enemy tomorrow.

No longer do any men
in my retinue swear,
gamble, or behave without valor.
They understand
we must be virtuous
if we are to be victorious.

Even though for the first time
I am surrounded entirely by men
all hours of day and night,
I never fear for my safety in the camp.
These men will protect me
as would my father.

They care for me
as does my mother.
I love them as my family,
and in some ways even more.

MEETING THE BASTARD

I know this mission to lift the siege
of Orléans will establish
my credibility should I succeed,
or end my days in armor
should I fail.
I try not to let the mounting pressure
rattle my boots,
but my stomach sputters
and I nearly retch my fears
onto the ground.

Five miles east of Orléans,
my convoy meets Count Dunois,
the Bastard of Orléans.
He governs the city
now under siege,
because his half brother,
the Duke of Orléans,
remains a prisoner of the English.

Dunois seems pleased to see us.
He marvels at the size of my army
and the great commanders
who stand beside me.

I am eager to fight,
to unburden the weight
of my first-ever battle,
but I see no enemy.

The evil man Talbot
I was told we came to fight
must be hiding like a coward
beneath his mother's skirt.
Dunois reads the puzzlement
in my eyes.

He explains that I was made
to approach his city from the east
so that the much-needed supplies
I have brought
might enter Orléans
by the one gate
not controlled by the English.

This was not the plan
my men and I agreed to.
We came to wage war,
not transport supplies.

Is this Dunois
an ally
or a boulder blocking our path?

The Bastard smiles as if he has
done me a favor.
"I and others,
who are even wiser than I,
advised you to take this route,
believing it was the safest passage."

I survey the great river before us.
"So we must pass over the Loire
to reach Orléans?"

The man nods.
"But unfortunately, the winds blow
in the wrong direction today,
and our ships cannot cross the river.
So we must wait."

Why did Dunois neglect to tell me
we were not headed for battle
after all my prayers
and preparation last night?
God told me to fight today.
And surely, He knows more
than any of Dunois's wisest captains.

Dunois smiles.
"I do apologize, dear Maid."

I am not sure I believe him.
I clasp my hands,
look up to heaven,
and pray hard
to the one leader
I will always abide.

A CHANGE OF WIND

April 29, 1429

I cross myself and say,
"Let us be on our way."

Dunois gestures to the river.
"Our boats cannot sail to Orléans
because of the wind."

I pat him on the arm.
"Do not worry about the wind."

As soon as these words
depart my lips, the wind switches
direction so that the ships
can move across the river.

Dunois falls to his knees
and kisses my hand.
"Please come with me into Orléans.
My people will rejoice
to meet La Pucelle."

I protest that I should
remain with my men.

But this man argues
almost as well as I do.
He implores me again
to enter his city,
as Orléans has been besieged
for over six months,
and the people
will be strengthened
for the fight ahead
if they can behold the miracle
that is the Maid.

I eventually acquiesce
but vow not to stay long
in Orléans,
for there is war to wage.

I do not want my courage
or that of my troops
to wither or wane.
For momentum can be lost
faster than the sun
vanishes before a storm.

ORLÉANS

Perched on the right bank of the Loire,
Orléans is a well-fortified city
with sturdy, thus far impenetrable walls
upon which twenty-one cannons mount.
It remains a bastion of hope for southern France.
Like chain mail under armor,
the city stands as our last line of defense.

Outside, towers, gates, and moats
were constructed to protect Orléans,
but just as the English stole our harvests
and set aflame our crops,
the ramparts have been sieged or destroyed.
Now all the bastilles are controlled
by the enemy.

The twenty thousand citizens of Orléans
harbored within her walls
have grown desperate
with starvation and fear.

But not today.
How the eyes of children
light up like torch fire
when wagons of grain
and wine and livestock
enter the city.
How they gaze
upon my countenance
as if they behold
the face of God.
I do not deserve
such a reception.
I have done nothing
to merit their love
yet.

BEFORE THE BATTLE OF ORLÉANS

I feel like a fatted calf in this city.
Spoiled and pampered,
I sleep in a soft child's bed
while my men tent outside the gates.

Confined, I put myself to task.
For three long days
I scope our enemy from the outer wall,
size up the English strongholds,
and seek out holes in their armor.
Because the English greatly outnumber us,
we will have several days of fighting
to reclaim Orléans.
So I develop a plan.

Before the battles begin,
I am asked to parade
through the streets of Orléans
on my white horse

in full armor,
bearing my standard.

The townspeople mistake me
for an angel.
They stroke my steed
and reach for my hand,
as though to touch me
is to feel something divine.

But really, I am
no different than them.
I may be sent by God,
but I am flesh and blood.

Underneath my armor
I am just a girl.

CAPTAINS

Every day I offer the English
a chance to lay down their arms.
But they just laugh
and call me whore,
a name they know hurts me most.
None of our male commanders
endures insult or harassment,
but tears often stain my pillow at night.
I do not understand why I alone
must be slandered.

●◆●

All the captains stand
when I enter,
as they would for a noble lady.
But clearly, I have been excluded
from a portion of their meeting
in Dunois's castle.
I must be viewed

as an unnecessary mascot in this war,
or worse, as a hefty chain
burdening their ankles.

I do my best to camouflage
any hurt or anger I feel
over having been left out,
especially because this mission
was initiated by me
and would not otherwise exist.
I might have expected
that Dunois and the captains we paid
would scheme behind my back,
but La Hire and the Duke of Alençon
also sit at the table.

To feel betrayed
by one's friends
is both unexpected and painful,
like falling on your back
so hard you lose your breath.

Count Dunois acts as though
I have missed nothing of import.
He informs everyone
that the English have called in
reinforcements.
Still a day's march from Orléans,
they are led by the dreaded Fastolf,

the English captain
who commanded the crushing defeat
of the French army at Verneuil.

When the group disassembles,
I disclose to Dunois
that after days surveying
our enemy's position,
I have devised
a plan of attack.

The Bastard smiles and thanks me,
promising to discuss
my strategy tomorrow.
But as I retire to sleep,
I cannot temper the feeling
that his words were merely
a pat on my head,
that Dunois sees me as a pet,
not an equal.

THE FIRST BATTLE
May 4, 1429

In my sleep, I smell smoke
so acrid my eyes water.
I believe I am dreaming
once again of the barn fire.

But when I snap awake,
the air tastes like gunpowder.
I hear cannons boom.
Somehow the fight began
without me this morning.

In my frenzy
to get to the battlefield,
I forget my standard.
It must be passed to me
through the bedroom window
while I sit astride my horse.

Why would Dunois wage war without me?
Why would he deceive me, *again*?

I gallop beyond the walls.
There is no battalion led by Fastolf,
just a small garrison of English soldiers
who struck out
from their stronghold at Saint-Loup
with an aim to run off my army
or kill my men,
whichever happens first.

As I join my troops,
La Hire hollers, "La Pucelle,
do you always arrive late
to the party?"

How can I be late
if no one invited
me to the battle today?

No one except God.
I raise my standard high.
"I am here now."

The Duke of Alençon
lifts his visor.
"We are losing and badly.
Our men could use
the courage of the Maid."

I gallop toward the fighting.
The ground smells of blood,
excrement, and death.
I feel sick to my stomach.
Nevertheless, I march into the fray.

When I appear beside our men,
the French soldiers
see my fearless banner
and begin to fight
with renewed strength.
The battle's tide turns in our favor.

The English retreat into Saint-Loup,
a fort that used to be a monastery,
which they seized several months ago.

Ten long minutes of inaction.
Then a group of holy men,
without weapons or words,
stream out of Saint-Loup.
I command my men
not to harm the monks
and let them pass.

Within an hour, the English army
yields and deserts the rampart.
We reclaim Saint-Loup
and capture forty of their soldiers.

I count one hundred forty
dead Englishmen.
We have won our first battle;
still I weep for every lost soul.

When I learn later that
the monks I let escape unharmed
were just English soldiers
disguised in stolen monastic robes,
I swear to my men
that those blasphemous scoundrels
will not go free when next we meet.

ON THE BATTLEFIELD

I never felt at ease
in a kitchen,
in the stuffy confines
of house and hearth.
I have always been
a girl who needs air and sky,
who best sees heaven through
the trees and stars.

Although the brutality
of steel into flesh,
of men gasping for their last breath
and crying out in pain for God's release
shatters my heart,
I find that part of me is exhilarated
by the strategic planning of battles,
and the valor of knights.
To encourage brave Frenchmen
to fight for our country

feels like kneeling in church.
I have finally discovered something
for which I possess talent
that suits my soul.

STRATEGIZE

Forgiveness
comes easily when
the duke and La Hire bend knees
and, with the remorse of children
caught telling their first lies,
apologize
for not demanding
that I be included
in the strategy meetings
or informed about the first battle.

What do I advise
we do next?

I pull out a map
of the English camps
surrounding Orléans
and architect
our plan.

ASCENSION DAY
May 5, 1429

Today is Ascension Day,
a holy day that commemorates
the bodily rise of Christ into heaven.
We pray and fast and do not fight.

I dictate another letter to the English:

Men of England,
you have no right
to this Kingdom of France.
Abandon your strongholds
and go back to your country.
I am writing to you for the final time;
I will not write anything further.

P.S. I have sent my letters to you
in an honest manner,
but you are still holding my herald Guyenne.
If you are willing to send him back to me,
I will return you some of the men

captured at the fortress of Saint-Loup,
for they are not all dead.

I roll up the parchment and
pin it to an arrow.
An archer launches
the scroll to the English.

The English may act
as if because I am a woman
I am of no consequence,
a drop of rain easily ignored
amidst a violent storm,
but they read my words.
And they return my herald.

YOU CAN RUN, BUT YOU CANNOT HIDE

May 6, 1429

The signs from God
I promised the council in Poitiers
etch themselves victoriously
upon the ground
as each day we capture
another enemy stronghold.

This morning the English
ran away from their fort
at Saint-Jean-le-Blanc,
so fast their fires still smolder.

But Les Augustins, which obstructs
the main road into Orléans,
remains a valued English rampart.

I advise that we strike directly
at the strongest part of Les Augustins,
so La Hire, the Duke of Alençon, and I

gather four thousand soldiers
and several hundred knights.

Because of our inferior numbers,
the other captains call this a suicide mission.
As if they fight against, not beside us,
these commanders try to block our way.

But the soldiers want to follow me,
for they believe God is on my side.
The other captains wear faces of sour milk
as they are forced to support my plan.

La Hire, the duke, and I
ride in the vanguard.
Swift and first with our lances,
we knock down everything in our path
like a tempest that breaks the dam.

Our enemy soon faces slaughter
and must retreat into the only bastille
still in English control,
the well-fortified Les Tourelles.

The English captains
Talbot and Suffolk had fresher troops
and a better position,

but neither believed we had the courage
to attack the bastille directly.

The battle won,
I jump down from my horse
and step on a *chausse-trappe*,
a small spike in the ground
designed to penetrate hoof or foot
and slow both infantry and cavalry.
But victory eases the pain,
so if my foot throbs, I barely feel it.

A council of the other captains
decides that the army should rest
while they send out spies
and devise subterfuge.
It is unthinkable to these men
that our smaller army
could win another direct battle
against the English.

But I have prayed,
and God tells me we should
strike tomorrow.

This time Dunois
urges his other captains
to cede to my better counsel
and ready their troops.

GIRL IN CHARGE

I know that I am
but a humble blade of grass
amidst a great field of soldiers.
And that all our success
comes from God.

But a smile rises
like the sun across my lips.
I take pride,
as I imagine one who designs
a grand cathedral does
when he gazes at his golden spires
crowning the sky—
for I am a seventeen-year-old girl
who now leads thousands of men.

It seems beyond impossible,
yet because of Him
I am.

ONE BATTLE MORE

There remains only
one rampart to capture,
Les Tourelles,
and I will make good
my promise—
Orléans will be free
of the English.

The security of this city
will pump my country
full of blood
and vigor
and belief.

Exhilarated over tomorrow's
important battle,
I find sleep eludes me.
Instead I am visited
by thoughts
of my sister.

Catherine
would have no place
in this army
were she alive.
Yet I feel her presence
as surely as the rain
that rattles the roof
of my tent.

My sister looks
down from heaven
and blesses me
with strength.

THE SIEGE OF LES TOURELLES: THE DECISIVE BATTLE OF ORLÉANS

May 7, 1429

First light slowly climbs
the English tower.
Six hundred of their soldiers wait
in ready defense from the south.
We storm the rampart
from multiple vantages.
Our men, like wild horses unbound,
charge the wall in every direction.

The English fight with axes,
maces, and even their fists,
desperate vermin
trying to beat us down
as we top the bulwark.
Gunpowder blasts
and cries of the fallen
accompany the fighting

like a dirge of kettledrums
and mourning doves.

God told me an English arrow
will pierce my flesh
during this battle.
I bury the thought
like a bad dream.

I hoist up my banner
to embolden the soldiers.
No matter what,
I will stay beside the men,
so they keep good heart
and never retreat.

Raising the scaling ladder
against the redoubt,
I climb nearly to the top
when the steel enters me, sharper
than I expect, the pain
so stifling I cannot breathe.

The arrow lodges
between my neck and shoulder
and cuts straight out my back.
I want not to weep, but I do.

A squire carries me to safety.
My wound is tended with cotton
and a poultice, but the injury runs deep.
Angelic voices sing me to sleep,
soft hymns to calm my suffering.

When I wake,
I know without being told
that my men have lost ground.
Dunois and the other leaders
summon the troops
back to camp.

I grab my standard,
wriggle into my light armor,
and wince as I mount my horse.
It feels as if I carry an ox
on my shoulders.

I humbly ask that God
grant me strength.

My pain breezes away
like clouds that obscure,
then reveal, a mountaintop.
I stand tall.

I ride high above the trench,
so both my men
and the English can see me.

The enemy trembles,
for now
even they believe
I am sent by God.

The English scatter
back into their holes like mice.
Our men assault the bulwark
with divine fervor.
Overrun, the southern fortress falls.

Dunois launches a second attack
from the north.
His men storm a gap in the Bridge Gate.
Now French troops pinch both sides.
Our terrified enemy offers
almost no resistance.

As a final measure,
we torch a boat
beneath the connecting drawbridge.
I scream to the English commander
to submit to the King of Heaven.
But he stubbornly refuses to surrender.

He urges his skeleton troop
across the crumbling, blazing bridge.
The wooden beams collapse,
and his few remaining men
plunge into the river.
The English soldiers cannot swim
in their heavy armor.
They drown like ships
ravaged by cannon fire.
I weep for their souls.
Why must victory
come at the cost
of so many dead?

We ride back to Orléans victors,
still in only three days of warfare
thousands of men perished.

I try to celebrate
with our troops.
But my smile feels
like a set of false teeth.
As we parade through town,
my pain returns,
only now,
it is a thousand times deeper.

AFTER THE FINAL BATTLE

I have never heard
so many church bells.
They ring, loud as cannons,
to proclaim God's victory.

The citizens prepare a victory feast
large enough to feed the whole city.
The other captains and men-at-arms
eat ravenously as if they are dogs
that have gone weeks without food.
I eat, as I always do, very little,
just some bread dipped in wine—
the food of Christ's last supper,
the nourishment of his body.

The remaining English troops
stand armed outside Orléans's main gate.
It is Sunday, so the rules of warfare
prohibit armies from attacking.
Captains Talbot and Suffolk came to see

if we will fight or negotiate.
We will do neither,
but allow the English army to retreat
without harming a single soldier.

Most of their men withdraw
to the city of Meung;
a lesser number fall back to Jargeau.
With defeat and fear stuffing their armor,
the men flee in such haste,
they leave behind valuable artillery,
arrows, and gunpowder,
which we happily procure.

I rest for two days
to allow my wound to heal,
or at least stop bleeding
when I twist and turn,
before moving on
to the second and perhaps
even more important part
of my mission.

DAUGHTER OF GOD, GO, GO, GO

May 9, 1429

Dunois, La Hire, the Duke of Alençon,
and I trek ninety miles south
to meet with the dauphin.

When we arrive,
Charles is closeted in his private quarters
with his confessor and advisers
like he fears the sun.
I vanquish custom and courtesy
and do not wait for the dauphin
to allow me entrance into his chambers,
but fall to my knees and beseech him
to come as quickly as he can
to receive a worthy coronation.

I explain to Charles
and his entourage
that yesterday I was told
by the King of Heaven,

daughter of God, go, go, go,
and I will be your aid.

I clutch Charles's hand
and humbly request of him
money to rebuild his army,
as the battles at Orléans
depleted both supplies and soldiers.

Both God and the people
stand behind me now
and rejoice in the knowledge
that the dauphin
has beaten his enemies.
I beg of Charles
on bended knee
that he allow me to take him
to the city of Reims
to be crowned.

CLEARING THE ROAD TO REIMS

As is his way,
the dauphin hesitates
like a man who dips his toe,
many times testing the water,
before immersing himself in a bath.
Charles asks that I clear
a path for him to Reims.
Too many cities are loyal
to the English between
here and the city of coronation.
The dauphin will grant me money,
supplies, and additional men,
but I must reclaim his towns.
The triumph at Orléans alone
does not assure him
that he should be crowned.

I am eager to obey
and would enter battle
tomorrow,

but what I need
cannot be provided quickly.

Charles appoints
his cousin the Duke of Alençon
to lead his forces
instead of me.
If I am not to serve
at the army's helm,
at least it is the duke,
my dear friend,
who steers.

MORE PROOF

The dauphin says
he believes
that I am
sent by God,
yet he requires
more assurance.

I do not doubt
that he is the one
true king of France,
but I wonder
if sometimes
he does.

It is as though
Charles requires
heavenly hosts
to fly overhead
and proclaim
in glorious

and melodic unison
that he is
king.

Perhaps it is easier
for others
to believe in you
than it is
to believe
in yourself.

AS I COMMAND

I travel to Saint-Laurent,
where the Duke of Alençon
makes his home,
to discuss our strategy.

The duke tells me upon
my arrival that he cedes
all military decisions to me.

With the exception of La Hire,
the other leaders,
even those who believe in me
like Dunois,
have doubted my strategies
as though I know not
a sword from a shield.
But not the duke.

I suggest that we strike first
at Jargeau,
where some of the English troops
holed up after their defeat
at Orléans.

The duke wholeheartedly
concurs.

NOBLE WOMEN

The Duke of Alençon's wife, Jeanne
(we share the same name),
whose father is the imprisoned Duke of Orléans,
welcomes me into her home
as if we are old friends,
never once acting as though
I do not belong
among nobility.

Likewise, the duke's mother,
Mary of Brittany,
treats me with kindness and respect.
She has porcelain skin
and eyes like a cloudless sky.
Mary of Brittany makes me ache
for my own mother
with more pain
than did the arrow that pierced my flesh.

As comfortable as I have become
living among soldiers,
the gentility of these women
reminds me that I have long preferred
dwelling among the flowers of the garden
rather than the crops in the field.

Jeanne and Mary stroll
with me through the estate grounds.
Unlike my father's,
the duke's garden does not grow
vegetables to feed his family
but exists like a statue or a tapestry
for the sake of loveliness alone.

I inhale lavender and mint,
dust my fingers in morning dew,
and listen to leaves chatter in the wind.
I will paint a picture of this spring
to hold forever in my mind.

Jeanne grasps my hand and confides
that she fears for her husband,
because the duke is only twenty-three
and already spent five years as a prisoner.
Her father has been imprisoned
for almost thrice as long.
Jeanne could not bear
for her children to grow up

without knowing their father
or grandfather.

I bow my head and assure her
that I will keep her husband safe,
that God tells me
her husband will be unharmed
as long as he fights by my side.

With God's assurance and my vow,
Jeanne relinquishes her worry
like a knight unburdening himself
of his heaviest armor.

FRIENDS BECOME FAMILY

If the dark held terror or unrest
for me as a little girl,
my mother would sing hymns
to calm me.

I could not close my eyes
last night without seeing flames,
and I must have cried out in my sleep.

Even though I should be beyond
the age of needing a mother,
Mary and Jeanne sat by my bedside
and soothed me with tales
of the duke as a boy.
Mary held my hand
until I fell asleep
without fear.

A mother's comfort
is not a pair of childhood boots.
It is something
one never completely
outgrows.

RETURN TO THE FIGHT

As promised,
Charles raises the funds,
supplies, and men
so we can return to war.

Up until their defeat
at Orléans,
the English appeared
as invincible as lightning—
their every strike wounding us,
causing us to burn.
But I have thrown water
on the flames.
In Orléans,
I proved not only
that a girl
can lead an army.
I proved that we French
can win.

Now peasants and nobles alike
pick up pitchfork and sword
and march
beside me and the duke.

In this next phase of warfare
we will clear a path to Reims
for the dauphin
and reclaim French cities
occupied by the English.
Enemy armies and commanders
who fled Orléans,
who refused to surrender,
who failed to return
what has never belonged to them,
we will pursue and capture.

The duke and I chart our course
with the confidence of an emperor,
as if we feel able
to conquer the world.

MY REAL BROTHERS

An unexpected surprise—
Jean and Pierre show up
to join my army.

Jean squints
and examines my tunic.
He says I look different.

Pierre asks,
"Is it really you, Jehanne?"

I motion for my brothers
to sit and eat.

My eyes blur.
It is as though
with a blink of my lids
I have become two people,
the one in armor
who rides a warhorse

and a girl I can hardly remember,
seasoning stew
in a russet dress.

Jean and Pierre sit down awkwardly.
Their eyes drink in the camp—
soldiers at prayer,
men sharpening swords
and sipping wine.

Jean looks as perplexed
as a snake without a tail.
He cannot comprehend
how all these soldiers
do as I command.

Pierre informs me
that Mother is worried about me
and sent my brothers
to look after me.

Jean gestures to my shoulder,
still swathed in bandages.

I brush away his hand
before he pokes at my wound.
I explain that an arrow hit me,
but I am fine,
that God always protects me.

With a lift of his eyebrows
Pierre wonders why I limp.

I explain that in battle
I ride a horse
and hold my standard,
so the limp is of no consequence.

Pierre mumbles, his mouth
full of bread and sardines,
that Mother would hate
to see me hurt.

Jean empties his goblet of wine
before launching into a series of questions
that squeak and snarl
with disapproval.

Have my brothers come
to fight the enemy
or only to question me?
Because I need answer to no one,
except God and the dauphin.
But I resist saying this to them.

Jean kicks the dirt.
"I think being with these soldiers
has not been good for you."

Pierre's eyes widen
as he asks the question
that has been foremost
in both my brothers' minds—
Am I really La Pucelle,
sent by God
to save France?

HAPPY TO SEE THEM?

I have fallen so deeply
into my role of commander
and warrior, of standard-bearer
and emboldener of men,
it is as though I buried
Jean and Pierre's sister from Domrémy
on the field of my first battle.

My brothers reawaken
a part of me
that might best remain
in hibernation.
A farmer's daughter
does not lead an army.

I almost wish
Jean and Pierre had stayed
among Father's cattle and grain.
Yet I cannot deny my brothers

the honor of fighting
for God and country.

But if they have come to serve,
they must be soldiers
like all others
and understand that
I am a soldier and a leader
before I am their sister.
That here,
I am La Pucelle.

THE BATTLE OF JARGEAU
June 11–12, 1429

Today urgency courses through my veins
like a charging brigade.
I keep thinking about
how I am destined to die
before I am twenty
and how scarce little time
I have to crown Charles
and help defeat the English.

I expect no resistance
before we reach the city,
but the English leap out
from behind their fortifications
like evil ghouls
with enough fright and force
that my men fall back.

But I do not.
I lift my standard
and cry to my men

to have good courage.
Infused with purpose and optimism,
the French troops drive the English
inside their powder-packed towers
and the walls of Jargeau.

When night falls and the fighting ceases,
I send the English a letter
demanding surrender.
The English do not laugh at my words,
but they also do not retreat.

In the morning, we bombard Jargeau
until the town's walls
are pitted and damaged
like a face ravaged by pox.

We construct ladders and other assault tools
to scale the walls outside Jargeau.
I carry my standard into the ditch
and charge forward with the troops
to mount a siege ladder.
A rock shatters my helmet
and I tumble to the ground.
As soon as I regain breath,
I am on my feet screaming
that our Lord has doomed the English
and at this very hour, they will be ours!

The duke comes to attend me,
but I shout at him,
"Retire from where you are standing
or you will die!"
He moves immediately.
Five minutes later a French soldier
dies in the exact spot
I told the duke to vacate.
The duke lives, but another man
dies in his place.
My heart sinks like a cross of lead.
At least I have kept my promise
to the duke's wife.

I desperately search the field
for my brothers.
But dust and smoke
blanket my vision,
and I cannot see but twenty feet
beyond my horse.
I pray Jean and Pierre
still stand at the end of the day.

Just before night swallows the sky,
our troops redouble their efforts.
We reclaim the town of Jargeau
and take the English Captain Suffolk prisoner.

FATE

I ask my page
to scour the camp
and find Jean and Pierre.
I will not close my eyes
until I learn their fate.

The duke delivers
the news that my brothers
sleep like infants,
nestled fireside
shoulder to shoulder.
They looked so peaceful
he dared not wake them.

I would trade my best boots,
well, my second-best boots,
for restful sleep like that.
The excitement of battle
still races within my chest

like a bull prodded by a whip.
It is futile to close my eyes.

My untarnished banner
flaps and gleams
in the corner of my tent.
No matter how many battles
my standard faces,
it does not tatter or tear.
Like the French army,
it never fails me.

But I know I face a deadly fate
somewhere beyond these victories.
Like slow-moving smoke,
it seeps under the door and circles round my feet.
Right now, were I to run away
and leave behind all that I love,
desert my men and my mission,
could I spare my own life?
Or would that simply be
a different kind of death?

DAUGHTER OF GOD, GO, GO

We return to Orléans with prisoners
and another victory to great celebration.
No captain disputes my decisions.
Six thousand soldiers have joined
the army, and more enlist each day.
Lords, knights, squires, captains—
every sort of men-at-arms
lines the street, ready to fight for France.

Pierre and Jean strut like peacocks,
fan their feathers of pride.
They walk two steps behind
me and the duke
as we wave at the crowd
from our destriers.

Jean marvels at how
the people love me.

Pierre boasts to everyone
that I have courage enough
for my entire army of men!
I knew to keep fighting
when others would have lain back.

But God leads us.
Not I.

The duke touches my hand
and tells me I am too modest,
that I follow God's will,
but it requires great bravery to do so.

But I am no different
from any other soldier.

"You are remarkable, Jehanne."
The duke calls me by my name.
He smiles and trots off
to join Dunois and discuss tonight's feast.

My brother Jean grips
the bridle of my horse
as he raises one eyebrow
like an indictment.

But Jean misunderstands.
The duke is *chef de guerre*,
leader of the army.
He heeds my advice,
and that is all.

A NIGHT OF KNIGHTS

I do not always enjoy
the celebration after a battle won,
but this Loire Campaign
rescued French towns
from English captivity
and snared valuable
English captains as prisoners.
It merits some applause.

It feels good to emerge
from underwater
for a breath now and then,
to indulge in a night of laughter and levity
and remove my armor.

Tonight, I gleam
outside the arena of war.
Not mud-covered and manly,
I shimmer like a pretty girl,
like moonlight upon the lake.

The duke sits to my right
and La Hire hunches
beside me on the left.
Around the circular table
Dunois, Jean de Metz,
and all my commanders
toast one another's bravery
as if we raise glasses at a wedding.

My brothers received
no invitation to this feast,
as they are soldiers but not captains.
I could have included them
as my guests,
but I wanted a night of my own
to revel among my new brothers,
not be webbed in the past
by my old.

Amidst the merriment
the duke and I strategize.
With the English Captain Suffolk
behind bars, we believe
we should next pursue Talbot
with the ferocity of wild boars.
Talbot appears to be the heart
of the English army in this valley.

The Hedgehog disagrees.
La Hire says it is Fastolf
who lies at the center.
If we topple Fastolf,
all the trees
in the English forest fall.

FASTOLF

Fastolf is the feared captain
of the English.
But he is just a man,
and we have God
on our side.

It is rumored
he is but a day away
from us
and brings
so many fresh men,
we will be
crushed
like a skull in a vise.

CONFIDENCE

I confess
that these days
I have found the confidence
a farmer feels
in a well-watered crop,
for God is with me.

Still I try to remember
what is lost
when we win.
All men belong to God,
even the enemy.

What does not belong
to the English
is France.

REINFORCEMENT

I learn that the commander Richemont
approaches us from the south.
Richemont sided with the Burgundians
and because of his disloyalty
has been banished by the dauphin.
I, therefore, assume he is our enemy,
though rumors say he has come
to fight for our cause
against the English.

When Dunois, the Duke of Alençon, and I
ride out to meet Richemont,
I ask his intentions
and force him to swear
allegiance to Charles.
Richemont vows his loyalty.

I am glad Richemont
has come with his fresh troops
and high spirit.

He shines like a newly forged blade.
And now we outnumber
the English three to one.

SURRENDER TO THE MAID
June 16–17, 1429

The city of Beaugency
learns of Richemont
and does not want to fight,
but instead surrenders.
Its soldiers leave for Paris
with their lives, horses, and little else.

We learn that
English captain Fastolf
and his army of four thousand men
have gathered in the forest
between Beaugency
and the city of Patay,
ready for combat.

This battle may be the last
we need fight before
leading the dauphin to Reims.

Our men assume battle formation
and prepare for the enemy forces
to arrive against us.

But the English never come.

We move into the woods
to track the cowards down,
hoping no sleight of hand
awaits us.

DAUGHTER OF GOD, GO: THE BATTLE OF PATAY

June 18, 1429

God sends a stag to warn us.
Seven hundred English archers
were setting their stakes
and preparing to ambush our troops
with a rain of arrows
when our advance scouts
watched an enormous elk leap
from behind some brush
and disorient the archers.
They hollered at one another
and made a game of hunting the stag
rather than readying for battle.

Knowing their position,
we charge the English,
brandishing our sharpened steel.
A slaughter ensues.

The English are disorganized
and unprepared.
We pursue their army
to four miles outside Patay
and make swift our spurs
to capture or slay them
as they flee.

We snare Captain Talbot,
while the mighty Fastolf
turns on his heels
and retreats.

It is estimated
that nearly all four thousand English
are killed or taken prisoner.
We lose less than twenty men.
Patay becomes the decisive
victory of the Loire Campaign.

With my presence on the battlefield,
we always win.

Now we must crown the king.

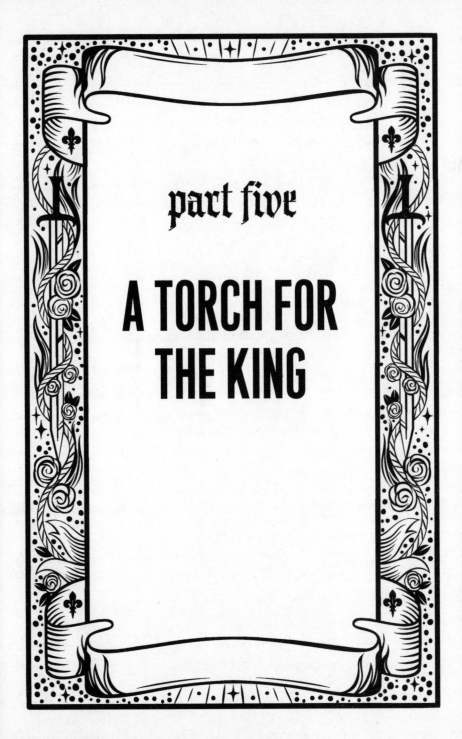

part five

A TORCH FOR THE KING

RETRIEVING THE DAUPHIN

June 24–27, 1429

Like sun obscured
by clouds, trees, mountains, and mist,
things are rarely singular
and clear at court.
The king's councillors advise
whatever benefits
their selfish interests.

After waiting a week
to see the dauphin, I learn that
Charles fears that not all the towns
along the route to Reims
are on his side.
I promise him that the cities
that have not surrendered
will do so without a fight.
And further, when he is crowned king
in Reims, it will be difficult
for the English to harm him
because he will have been anointed

with the holy oil
that will garner him
his people's full support.
He tells me he needs time
to consider my words.

I wish I had my mother's fortitude
of patience and tolerance.
Like an evergreen in winter,
she could withstand weeks
waiting for my father's return
and never shed a needle of complaint.

I pray for Charles to follow
the clear and righteous path.

THE WAY TO THE CROWN

The dauphin finally decides
to follow me to Reims.

We pass through Auxerre
without resistance.

The next city on our route,
where we expect to rest
and feed our troops, is Troyes.

But even after several parleys,
the people of Troyes offer no surrender.
Their defiance bricks a wall of doubt
between the dauphin and me.

We surround Troyes with ladders and artillery
and prepare to lay siege.
But before we release a single arrow,
an emissary is sent out.
In a parade of war and weaponry,

we pass in relative peace through the city gates.
Troyes kneels to the real ruler of France.

Last on our route to Reims
is Châlons,
which kindly welcomes us
like Auxerre,
without resistance.

On the horizon
the anointing place,
the holy cathedral,
the city that crowns kings—
Reims.

THE NOTRE-DAME CATHEDRAL AT REIMS

How do I describe a place
more beautiful than any
I have ever beheld,
ever imagined?
Think of roses
the size of small clouds
etched in colored glass.
Envision white vaulted towers
piercing the sky like organ pipes
that sing heaven's praise.

I clutch the hand of the duke,
quite overwhelmed,
then fall to my knees
and cross myself.
"Glory be to God!"

I weep and weep.
Tomorrow the dauphin
will be crowned king of France.

The second part of my mission
will be complete.

THE KING AND THE MAID

Some say it is improper
for me to stand beside
the blood royal,
even if
I am sent by God.
I was born a peasant
and a female.
I should not be allowed
inside the cathedral
when a king is anointed.

I am a weed
among the lilies.
Aberrant, I should be plucked
and discarded.
I served my purpose,
cleared a path to the holy pond,
laid waste to the English insects
threatening the king's lands.

But God knows better
than self-interested nobles
who shall pray at His altar.
Weed or lily,
I am a soldier of the king
and a soldier of the King of Heaven.
And I will stand
where God commands.

I fear not
nobles, clerics,
or the consequences of disregarding
the inferior position of my sex,
though some whisper
that perhaps I should.

CROWNING THE KING

July 17, 1429

Eight hundred soldiers progress
to the cathedral.
The sun shines brightly
through the magnificent rosette
spraying coins of colored light
on the marble floor.
The congregants wear bejeweled
garments of the finest cloths and furs.
La Hire sports a red velvet cape
strung with hundreds of silver bells
that jangle and clang as he moves
and announce his presence.
I have donned my armor
and carry my standard.
The king wears only a simple shift
until he is anointed and crowned,
as is the ceremonial rite.
He and I lead the procession
into the cathedral.
Behind us stride

the four appointed guardians
of the chrism, followed by
Dunois and the Duke of Alençon,
who carry Charles's crown and scepter.

When the dauphin reaches the altar,
he prostrates himself,
as does the archbishop.
Then Archbishop Renault rises
and dabs the holy oil on Charles's
head, chest, shoulders, elbows, and wrists—
the points of intelligence, passion, and command—
and says, "I anoint you for the realm with holy oil!"
The king replaces his simple shift
with anointed regalia and robe.
Renault prays that the king
prove himself worthy of the power
with which he has been entrusted.

The whole congregation yells, "Noel!"
over and over triumphantly.
I fall to the floor and wrap my arms
around my sovereign's feet.

So many bells ring,
it sounds as if
every angel in heaven
praises God together.
It feels as though

all the cannons on earth
fire at once.
A most magnificent cacophony
of celebration.
The whole of France
echoes with joy!

FAMILY REUNION

My parents traveled from Domrémy
along with several others from my village
to be in Reims for the coronation.
They were, of course, not permitted
inside the cathedral.

Mother slowly digests
the luxurious room
I have been given.
She eyes the tapestries and finery.
She gazes with awe at the extravagant silks,
velvets, and furs upon my dressing table
She hugs me tight.
"We are all so proud of you."

My father motions
for me to sit down,
as if nothing has changed
and I must do as he commands.
I pay him respect and find a chair.

There are so many
things I long to say to my parents,
but I fear they would not understand.
How could they?
There is a chasm of difference
between the girl before them
and the daughter they raised.

We shuffle our feet,
awkward as strangers.
It is as though time and distance
have left us without a common tongue.

Jean breaks the silence
and boasts about his valor
on the battlefield.

Pierre does not speak
of himself but brags about how
I was hit on the head by a boulder
yet jumped back onto my feet
as if nothing had happened.

Mother looks as if she might faint.

I explain to her
that God protects me.
But worry remains
on her face like a bruise.

I will always
be her little girl.

Father scratches behind his ear
and asks: Did all that praying
in the fields and chapel
have to do with crowning the king?

I nod.
Mother examines me closely,
memorizing my freckles
as if she fears
she will never see me again.

She knows I will not, I cannot
be returning to the village with them.
She wonders with both
the concern of a parent
and the curiosity of a follower:
What comes next?

ONE STAYS, ONE GOES

Jean returns to Domrémy
with my parents.
He kisses me quickly
on both cheeks,
impatient as a hound
held back from the hunt.
Jean never seemed
to enjoy farmwork,
but apparently
he likes standing
in my shadow even less.

Pierre pleads with Father
to allow him to remain at my side.
As he steps away from Jean,
I notice how tall
Pierre has grown.

After Mother, Father,
and Jean depart,
Pierre asks me
if I ever think about
Catherine.
He says her husband, Marc,
walks the village,
lost as baby bird
fallen out of a tree.

Tears pool in my eyes.
Yes, I think about
our sister.
I often feel that Catherine
rides straddled behind me
on my horse,
steadying me
on the battlefield.
She urges me
to lift my standard
when my arm grows weary.
And when I most fear death,
the knowledge
that I will see
Catherine and her baby
brings me great comfort.

She is the one
member of our family
who has never held me back
and never will.

Pierre smiles and nods.

Perhaps
my younger brother
will support me now
as did and would my sister.

WHAT COMES NEXT?

God remains surprisingly silent,
not even a whisper
of my next mission or move.
But I need not announce
this to king and country
or my men-at-arms.
My ultimate goal
is to liberate France from her oppressors,
to rid my country of the English,
and to restore peace
between the civil factions.

The iron blazes,
so strike, I say.
Attack Paris
before the English bring
thirty-five thousand fresh troops
across the channel
and fortify the capital.
Let us march on Paris

and take back our country now,
while the tide and momentum
ride with us.
Our fire ought rage and burn.
Now is not the time to sit back
and negotiate.
Now is the time to act.

But Charles stops the carriage,
halts the horses.
He allows French flames to cool
and barely keeps aglow
the royal embers.

We could destroy all enemies
in our path right now.
But instead
we kick around
in our own dust.

CHARLES'S TOUR
August 1429

For more than a month
the king tours
his newly recovered lands,
greeting his subjects,
feasting and celebrating.
He signs a truce
with the Duke of Burgundy
that prevents me from waging war.
In turn Burgundy promises
not to reinforce Paris.

Although we honor
the agreement,
the Duke of Burgundy
never intended to uphold
his end of the bargain.
The duke still smarts,
as if he nurses a fresh wound,
from King Charles's involvement

in the murder of his father.
He neglects to acknowledge that
his father, John the Fearless,
was a horrible and spiteful man,
and the Duke of Burgundy
benefited greatly from his father's death.

Two more weeks
King Charles dallies
as our enemies
grow in number and strength.
Charles thinks
war with these snakes
can be avoided.

Only after the Duke of Burgundy
and the English Duke of Bedford
taunt us with a cruel letter
does the king allow
me and the Duke of Alençon
to enter the fray.

But our army
is greatly diminished now.
We are like a hand
with only three fingers.
Many of our men have deserted
because they have not been paid.

Or they must tend to their harvest.
Or they believe that their sovereign
or their God no longer fights beside them.

We should not have delayed.

FRIENDS AND ALLIES ABANDON US

Finally able to strap on armor
and hoist my standard,
I decide we should still
attack Paris.
If we recapture the capital
from the English,
King Charles can assume
the true throne of France.

Forty days ago,
with the momentum of victory
as a tailwind puffing our sails,
great commanders to steer each ship,
and a fleet of soldiers,
reclaiming Paris
would have been
a stroll in the sun,
but we now face a trudge
through muck and murk.

All this time of truce
allowed our enemies
to fortify the capital
and ship in fresh troops.

More devastating,
the great commanders
who fought with me
in Orléans and the Loire Campaign—
Dunois, La Hire, Richemont,
even my first supporter, Jean de Metz,
have returned home to govern their cities.

The Duke of Alençon and my brother
alone remain to fight by my side.

Losing my friends and allies
feels like I have been stripped
of my sword, standard, and horse.

For the captains take with them
troops, supplies,
and much of our spirit.

SAINT-HONORÉ GATE, PARIS

September 8–9, 1429

The Duke of Alençon and I
survey the Parisian defenses
for over a week.
Bulwarks front the gates.
Houses next to the walls have been destroyed
and gunpowder weapons mounted.
Stones, cannonballs,
and a great moat and trench
circle the wall.
The English army of over nine thousand men
have dug in their sharpened stakes
and strewn *chausse-trappes* on the ground.
It has all been done to intimidate us.

After careful consideration,
we determine that
the weakest point of entry
is the Saint-Honoré Gate
on the Seine's right bank.

We bombard the walls
with cannons and gunpowder,
then throw wood, carts, and barrels
to clog up the moat
so we may cross into Paris.

The fighting, both muddy and violent,
slogs and exhausts.
We are only the bones
of the army we amassed in Orléans
and are greatly overpowered
by the English weaponry and men.

An arrow slices
through my thigh.
I fall back into the moat,
unable to lift myself
or my standard.
God did not warn me
I would be wounded
in this battle.
God has not spoken
to me at all.

My page raises up my banner,
but then an arrow cuts him down
at the thigh. He continues
to move forward with the standard
until a second arrow catches

him between the eyes
and mortally wounds him.
I weep beyond tears.
I cannot see the Duke of Alençon
and fear that I have broken
my promise to his wife,
and he is lost like my page.

The fighting continues
for four more hours.
I yell to give my men hope,
but my voice
cannot be heard
over the enemy cannons.

"RETREAT!" is called.

Pierre carries me back to camp,
as I cannot walk.
We have been defeated.

How can this be?
I did not think we could lose.
I thought God was always
on my side.

SHOULD WE CONTINUE?

Because we lost a battle
for the first time,
even more of the army
deserts me.
But defeat does not mean
I will turn in my standard.

When I first learned to sew,
I pricked my finger
as often as I stitched an even hem.
But instead of tossing in
my needle and thread,
I worked until mastery.
I never gave up
and will not now.

In fact,
this loss
fuels my desire
to win.

with a passion
so intense
my cheeks burn *rouge*.

A CHANCE TO FIGHT BACK

I beg the king for troops
to regain Burgundian territories,
but he is like a fat cat,
reluctant to move
from his spot in the sun.

Finally, King Charles capitulates
and sends me to La Charité
on the border of Burgundy.
He provides me with mercenaries,
soldiers who fight
not for king and country,
but for money.
It is a long and brutal siege,
and the winter is colder
than the devil is cruel.
When the king neglects
to pay the army,
they abandon their posts
and weaponry and me.

I am left with but a few loyal supporters.
And we cannot hold.

God finally speaks to me
through the snow and storm and wind and ice.
But instead of promising victory,
God tells me:
Jehanne, you will be taken prisoner
before Midsummer Day.
That is June 21,
less than half a year from now.
I have so little time
to capture Paris
and save France.

I gather another small force of my own,
a few hundred soldiers,
with the aid and finance
of my dear friend, the Duke of Alençon.
Together we ride into the town
of Melun, just south of Paris,
ready for battle
and eager for triumph.

Our feelings must inspire the populace.
They give up their allegiance to Burgundy
and pledge loyalty to Charles
as the true king of France.
There is no fight.

Disappointment washes over me
like water smothering a fire.
I so wanted a victory on the battlefield.
After loss and delay,
I ached to taste glory again.

DU LYS AND NO TAXES

Charles VII's coffers run dry
as a field of ash.
But even though the king
may lack money
and the ability to provide me with troops,
he grants me something else,
something as empowering
as a wind that sails ships—
he assigns me a coat of arms.
My entire family receives this.
Along with this honor comes
a title, *du Lys*, which means "of the lily."
This title makes me,
a girl who was born a peasant,
now a noblewoman.
This is practically unheard of.
Only a king has the divine right
to turn a peasant into a nobleman.
There is no greater gift.
Also, the king grants

that my village, Domrémy,
and the nearby town of Greux
will be tax-exempt forever.
I imagine the joy
this will bring my family and friends,
especially my father.
He will have to tally the taxes no more!

REALITY

The Duke of Alençon
gifts my brother a sword
with our family's new coat of arms
engraved on the handle.
Pierre jabs and slices at invisible enemies
like he used to thrash the air
with branches from our willow tree.

I ask Pierre
if he misses home,
if he wishes he had returned
with Mother and Father and Jean,
as we have not won a battle
since they left.

I wonder if he still believes
his sister Jehanne
is La Pucelle.

He regards me
as if a flock of geese
just flew out of my mouth.
He regrets nothing.
He has always
believed in me.
He knew I was destined
for greatness
even before I left Domrémy.
Anyone with two eyes
and half a wit
could see I was special,
chosen by God.
And now that King Charles
has made our family noble,
who could question
the purity of my mission?

Somehow Pierre speaks
the exact words I need
to nourish the place inside me
that feels hollowed with doubt.

He pats my arm.
"But you are human
like the rest of us,
and sometimes
even you will fail."

I stare out the castle window
at the sky twisted pink and violet
like *betoine* and lavender
smudged amidst the clouds.

I confess to my brother
that sometimes
I question whether one minute
I will wake
and find myself
lying in the grass beyond our barn,
all this having been
a lovely dream.

Pierre assures me
all I have seen and done
is real.

WINTER AND DREAMING OF WAR
1430

Treading back and forth on the carpet,
I pace more than I skirmish.
Wars waged only inside my head.

La Trémoille, the king's devious adviser
and no friend of mine,
keeps me at his family château
thirty miles upriver from Orléans,
away from the king
away from the duke
away from my brother
away from everyone
who might champion me
and help me amass an army.
Here I am useless and stagnant
as a puddle after a storm.
I might as well return to my village.
At least there I could help on the farm.

When I am ready to flay my own skin
just to escape boredom,
news arrives that citizens of Lagny
challenge the English
outside Paris in Compiègne.
With my new coat of arms,
the aid of the Duke of Alençon,
my old friend La Hire,
and my brother Pierre,
I raise a small troop of devotees.
We join the campaign
to reclaim the lands
surrounding Paris for the king.
It is a mighty and noble endeavor.
God must be on our side.

COMPIÈGNE
May 22–23, 1430

We arrive in the evening,
the crisp and marbled dusk
unfolding like a blanket
across the sky.
My four hundred
soldiers and archers
spend the night
sleeping as quietly as we can
in our armor.

Around nine in the morning
we charge forth,
gnashing our teeth,
and surprise the enemy
with our madness.
Because we are so outnumbered,
they do not expect us
to come at them
headfirst and headstrong,

a handful of bulls
fighting three thousand toreadors.

Though valiant, we cannot hold.
Additional troops
descend upon us from every direction,
hives of wasps so numerous
we cannot see them
to swat them away.
I call to my men to press on,
but they fall back.
My brother Pierre, the duke,
La Hire, and I
maintain the rear
as long and best we can.
But in the melee, even we
become separated from each other.

I back onto the bridge before Compiègne,
pressed on all sides by the enemy.
The city is gated by both
a thick wooden door
and an iron-grate portcullis.
When I reach the wall of Compiègne,
I find the door has been barred
and the portcullis slammed
down in front of me.
Neither can be opened.

I assume some of my men
found haven
within the city's walls.
The rest of us are trapped
on the bridge,
surrounded on all sides
by the enemy,
ensnared like hunters' prey.

We are doomed.

CAPTURED

May 23, 1430

Where is God?
Why did he not guide me,
warn me about this battle?
I do not understand.

Then I remember
that He told me I was to be captured
before midsummer.

A tug on my golden tunic
and I am thrown off my horse
by a man brandishing a crossbow,
a gleaming smile stretched across his face.
"Surrender, witch!" he cries.

I have no other choice.
I release my sword and standard.
I throw down my glove.
I do not move.
I wait for the nobleman

in charge to arrive,
lest I be ripped to pieces
by English or Burgundian soldiers
hungry to drink from my veins.
I seek the man who sees me
as a prize worth gold
rather than a blood sport.
The nobleman in charge,
named Jean de Luxembourg,
aids me to my feet like a gentleman.
He serves under the Duke of Burgundy.
At least I am not captured by the English.
Jean de Luxembourg binds my hands,
sets me upon a horse,
and hauls me to his castle as his prisoner.

THE CASTLE OF BEAULIEU

I know I will have a short stay
as prisoner in the castle of Beaulieu
because my king
will pay to have me released.
He has many English captains
to trade for my ransom,
and the Duke of Burgundy
will undoubtedly swap us one for the other
along with a few gold coins.

But weeks pass
and I remain in this tower
with my brother Pierre
and no word from King Charles.

It is not entirely unpleasant here.
However, being a prisoner
is a joy to no one.
I hope the negotiations hurry along.
I should like to kneel in prayer at mass,

gallop through meadows on my horse,
feel the sun simmer upon my face,
and hear the wind rush swiftly at my back.

MY LITTLE BROTHER

The guards escort my brother
to my cell most afternoons.
Pierre is not much happier
to be a prisoner than I am.
Locked in this castle,
he and I exchange more words
in one month
than we have in all our years
growing up.

My brother jests that
the army rations tasted like mud,
but the chef here serves
food still crawling in the bowl.
He is not sure which is worse.
He salivates, dreaming about
Mother's rabbit stew.

Pierre leans back in his chair
and confides that he once caught

Jean and Hauviette
frolicking in the rafters of the barn
without half their clothing.
I slap his arm and scold him
for not averting his gaze.

Pierre rolls his eyes.
My brother and Hauviette
are betrothed.
For such a worldly girl,
I can be as naive as a newborn foal.
But just because I am a virgin
does not mean I do not understand.
Besides, what does Pierre know
about love and women?
About as much as Father Pasquerel,
I suspect.

When I think there can be
no more to learn from or about
my younger brother,
the guards step into the hall
and Pierre whispers
that we must devise
a plan for my escape.

My eyebrows arch.
But what about his captivity?

He says not to worry
about him.
I am the one
the enemy is after,
I am the one
who must be free.

ESCAPE

As if I am merely a sleeping invalid,
when the guards change shifts,
for a few minutes I go unwatched.

I flip up a lose plank
and burrow beneath the floorboards.
An oversize mouse in a hole,
I try not to squeak or move.

When the new guards arrive,
the men wonder
if I am a sorceress
and have made myself disappear.
They scurry about the castle
in panic and terror,
scared they might encounter a witch,
and equally afraid of the consequences
should they fail to find me.

With the chaos I create,
I nearly escape to the freedom
of grass and sky.
But the porter
hears the jangle of his stolen keys
when I try to unlock
the outer door of my cell.

I receive a slap on the wrists
like a naughty child.

But what prisoner
would not wish to escape?
And I have never been
good at waiting.

Jean de Luxembourg shakes his head.
Now he will have to keep me
in a higher tower,
one seventy feet off the ground,
one from which I dare not escape.

THREE GOOD LADIES

In July I am moved
to the tower in the castle Beaurevoir,
where Jean de Luxembourg and his family reside.
It may be higher and more remote
than the first tower in which I was imprisoned.
It may more difficult to escape from
than Beaulieu, but it is far better
because of three ladies,
the lord's aunt, wife, and stepdaughter,
all named Jeanne.

The ladies treat me as a guest,
and more importantly,
after listening to me
they believe my mission is divine,
that I have done no wrong
and should be set free.

Jeanne, the Demoiselle of Luxembourg,
my captor's aunt, from whom

Jean de Luxembourg will inherit
all his land and money,
regards me like a daughter.
She entreats me to eat something.
It pains her to watch me waste away.
She believes that if everyone knew
how thin and frail I was and what a great warrior,
they would know for certain
I am heaven-sent.

I start to weep.
I cannot bear the thought
of remaining a prisoner
any longer than I already have.
If I am turned over to the English,
I may never be free.

The Demoiselle clasps my hand
and promises I will not
be turned over to the English.
Her nephew is reasonable.
He will return me to my king.
He will do what is right.
Or he will be disinherited.

SEEING BEYOND WALLS AND WAR

As I am a noble lady,
often no guards attend us
when the three Jeannes
visit me in the tower.
Because this is a home,
not a prison,
we might almost pretend
that we chat in a parlor,
not a cell.

The lord's aunt inquires
about my village, my family.

My voice cracks
like ice on a warm afternoon
when I speak
of how much I miss
my mother and Catherine.

Since my capture,
I would give anything
to be back in Domrémy,
spinning and mending,
praying in the chapel and fields.
Right now, I would give up fighting
for freedom.

The stepdaughter of my captor,
who is only a few years younger than I am,
but, unlike me, looks dew-kissed
as the first bloom of spring,
wonders when I last saw my mother.

Briefly, in Reims,
over a year ago, I explain.
But at that time
all I had washed my face with
was success.
I could not imagine needing her then.
Right now, I navigate a cave without light,
I feel certain my mother
could help me find my way.

DEATH OF HIS AUNT

A dreadful thing happens—
my best champion here,
the person most able
and willing to help
(because the king
seems to have forgotten me),
the noble lady,
the Demoiselle,
the aunt of Jean de Luxembourg,
who believes in La Pucelle
and would insist that her nephew
free the Maid,
dies.

So now my fate
lies in the hands
of men.
Heaven
help
me.

NO GOOD RANSOM

Charles, the king of France,
who at one time supported me
as if I were his daughter,
never offers to pay my ransom.
And Lady Jeanne, the wife of my captor,
informs me that my friends
La Hire and the Duke of Alençon
cannot offer enough ransom money
to satisfy the Duke of Burgundy.
So I will not be released
to my friends or allies.

The English offer
ten thousand francs for me
and promise to try me
by a council of French clerics
from the University of Paris.
They say it will be
somewhat like the council
I faced in Poitiers.

I want to believe
this trial will be like Poitiers,
and so does Lady Jeanne,
but we know better.
If the English hold sway,
my fate is predetermined.

I feel the castle cave in,
entombing me forever.
My worst fear becomes realized.
I am sold to the English.

BRUISED, BUT NOT BROKEN

I do not like to hear
church bells and skylarks
sing out morning songs
yet not see them with my eyes.
I do not like to smell
freshly baled hay
or autumn leaves after rain
but not touch them with my hands.

I do not wish to waste
a good length of rope
that appears in my cell
like a gift from God,
when I could try to climb
out a window with it,
even if it is far too short
and I nearly fall to my death
leaping with it.

I do not break a single bone,
even though I tumble
at least fifty feet
into the tower's dry moat
just below my prison window,
with not a tree limb or bush
or bed of flowers
to break my fall.

It hurts to fall.

Once again
I do not escape.

It hurts to fail.

I do not eat, drink, or move
for two full days.

I did not, would not,
try to kill myself,
even if death
is preferable
to imprisonment,
for suicide is a sin.

Let me be clear.
I tried to escape.

THE VOYAGE TO ROUEN

November–December 1430

Like a caged bird with
clipped talons and muzzled beak,
I am pulled along

in an iron jail,
a prisoner peering out of
an open wagon.

We traverse icy
marshes, pass through English and
Burgundians towns.

People gape and shout,
"Tramp! Sorceress! Whore!" They spit,
kick mud in my eyes.

It rains, sleets, ever
damp. My teeth chatter and clang.
I am chained and cold.

◆

Six weeks on the road,
but at least I am outside,
not trapped in a cell.

I see the ocean,
water without end, as if
the sky fell to earth.

Waves blast the shore in
great smoky mists, then bubble
away. White rising

over deepest blue.
Only God could make clouds dance
upon the water.

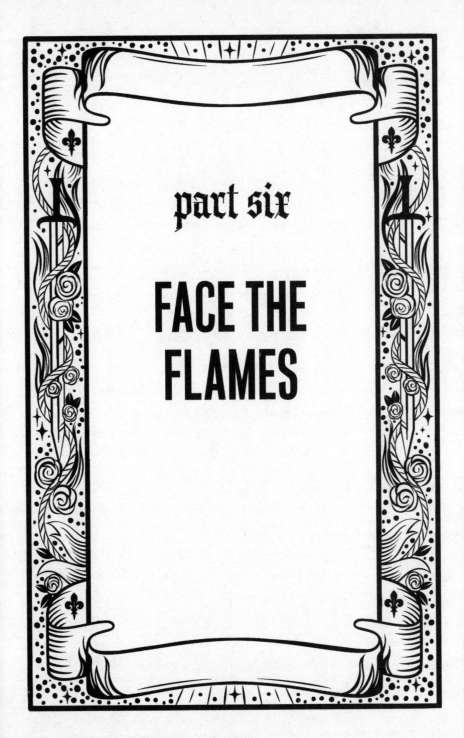

part six

FACE THE
FLAMES

ARRIVING IN ROUEN

December 23, 1430

Throngs of people
crowd the streets,
many in garments
more threadbare
than anyone
in my village wears.
The mob pushes and prods,
hoping for a glimpse of me.
Some people sneer and curse,
others applaud my capture.
Some peer at my face
with wide eyes
as frightened as my own.

We curl through
the narrow streets
slower than a man
who has lost his legs.
The buildings cram
one upon the next without

343

room to breathe.
They reach up
several stories high,
and are built of cob,
a mixture
of clay and straw,
laced with wood that zigzags
like a corset,
cinching the cob together.

Rouen might be a charming town
were it not for the sewage,
horse manure, and bodies packed
like sandbags during a flood.
Everything smells pungent—
nothing here escapes the nose.
I fear nothing here escapes.

MY NEW RESIDENCE

I live in the same place,
Bouvreuil Castle,
where the boy Henry VI lives,
the king of England
who tries to usurp Charles's throne.
I cannot imagine we reside
in similar quarters, however.

Although not underground,
my cell is as dark
as a room after dusk.
One small barred window
scatters a finger of light
onto the dirty floor.
The darkness depresses me
and draws out vermin and insects.

They chain me by the ankle
to a thick block of wood
at the foot of my bed.

They say it is because
I have twice tried to escape,
but I know it is just to punish me.
I want to cry out in despair,
but I hide my trembling lip.
The ankle fetter and its chain
weigh as much as heavy armor.
Cumbersome and painfully clamped
against my skin, the metal rubs and cuts
and greatly restricts my movement.
I feel as if I am slowly drowning.

What is worse is that at all times,
at least three English guards
remain inside my cell.
They shackle me without defense,
while the guards stand armed.
I speak little English,
but the foul things
the guards say require
no translation.
I am threatened, taunted,
and sometimes beaten.
I have no women attendants,
and no privacy.

My only solace
lies inside
my head and heart.

FIRE IN WINTER

The dream of fire returns.
Trapped alone in Father's barn,
a shower of flames
sets my hair ablaze.
The heat engulfs me
with its forked tongue.
My skin bubbles and blisters.
The floor opens fast beneath my feet,
drops me into the pits of hell.
I scream until I am hoarse
and awake.

I shiver with sweat,
my body soaked as if I were out
in a torrential rain.
My screaming scares my guards,
who now think me possessed
and call for reinforcements.
They fear I will hex them or worse.

If God started a fire in my cell
like he did that night in my father's house
when all the furniture was aflame,
that would *truly* terrify my guards.
A fire would also warm my trembling hands.
I could see my surroundings clearly
unshackled from a veil of darkness.
And I would be comforted
and bathed in the light of my Lord.
But no real fire ever appears.

DESPISED PRISONER OF THE ENGLISH

I stare at the thin brick of light
that slips through the window,
anything to keep my eyes off the guards.
When I remain as still as a stone,
the ruffians often forget about me.

I am told that the bishop of Beauvais,
Pierre Cauchon,
will preside over my trial.
Because he is French
and a bishop of the church,
will I have a fair trial here in Rouen?
Or does Cauchon serve the English,
and will he therefore be my enemy?

The voice inside my head counsels:
You must remain strong, Jehanne.
You will be weary.
You will want to quit.
But you must persevere.

"Will I be released from here?"
I ask aloud, gesturing to the cell door.

The guards laugh.

I try not to be frightened,
but I never know when I will be tormented
and when I will be left alone.

I quiet my mind, close my eyes,
but this time
the voice does not come.

LET ME BE WATCHED BY NUNS

Every day I beg my captors
to place me in church custody,
where I can be guarded by nuns.

Whether or not
I want to wear men's trousers
is not a question in this keep.
I am repeatedly harassed
and threatened with rape.
I wear two layers of hose
attached to my doublet,
strung with twenty cords,
each cord tied into three eyelets.
Although cumbersome to lace and unlace
when I need to use the latrine,
my clothing protects me from unwanted advances.

Bishop Cauchon finds this practice
of mine amusing but theatrical,
because he does not believe

that I am still a virgin.
Over a year I slept beside soldiers.
The bishop believes my soldiers
to be no more civilized than a pack of dogs.
In his eyes soldiers do what dogs do,
mount any, and all, available females.
Therefore, I must be corrupted.
But the bishop is wrong.

They drag
the English Duke of Bedford's wife
in to examine me.
For the fourth official time
I am found to be completely intact,
without doubt a virgin.

I plead again
to be removed
to a church prison
as is my right as a woman.
But like a vagrant child
begging for food on the street,
I am denied and ignored.

VISITORS TO MY CELL

During my first several weeks of captivity,
different dignitaries parade through my cell.
Most men are surprised and appalled
by my size and frailty.
They cannot believe
I am the great Maid of War.

Jean d'Estivet,
whom Bishop Cauchon assigned
to be the lead prosecutor at my trial,
reminds his guests
that I must then be a witch.

My trial will be conducted
as an inquisition.
I am accused of being a heretic and a witch.
Heretics are excommunicated.
Witches are burned at the stake.

Bishop Cauchon assembles
a council to hear my case.
I will have to defend myself
against sixty learned scholars of the faith,
all with the task of condemning me.

I shine my armor of endurance,
sharpen the steel of my mind,
and prepare for battle.

I overhear Jean d'Estivet
tell a dignitary that the friars
who thought my trial
unnecessary or unjust
were scratched from Cauchon's panel.
I am going to burn.

I remain hopeful.
The English and the assessors
may be on Cauchon's side,
but God is on mine.

WHOM I DO NOT SEE

My family and friends dare not
enter the city of Rouen
without my captors' consent.
As it is under English control,
they themselves
might be taken prisoner
or worse.

I am not once permitted
to see a friendly face,
not La Hire or the duke,
not Lady Jeanne of Luxembourg,
not my brother Pierre,
not any priest or confessor.

I am denied my request
to be visited by my mother.
I am forgetting the dimples
of her smile.

There is no one
for me to talk to,
the silence and isolation
enough to drive one
into a cave of despair.

Trapped in this cell,
I am lonelier than a tree
that has lost its leaves.
Only when I hear God
do I forget how deep and cold
is winter.

CHURCH BELLS

They say Rouen
is the city of two hundred bells.
Along with shifts of light on the floor
and the changing of my guards,
church bells keep the hours for me.
It is sanity to mark
the passing of time in prison.

I so loved the bells as a child,
I would fall to my knees in the fields
whenever the Saint-Rémy *cloches*
intoned their praise for God and France.

Once I was permitted
to go into the tower
to help the priest ring
for midday meal.
The bell's rope was heavy
and cumbersome,
especially for a small girl,

but I amazed Father Denis
with my strength and instinct.
It felt as if I had been
sounding the peal my entire life,
like I was born to ring out God's joy.

I hear my name
echo inside the bells.
Din-din, ding-dong,
clanging out Jehanne-Jehanne.

I press my hands against
the castle wall
when the two hundred bells
begin to clamor.
I allow their might
to thunder through my body.
Some days I wait, ear to stone,
for the comfort of their bellow.
And I match my beating heart
to their knell.

DO NOT REFUSE THE BISHOP

January–February 1431

The preliminary phase
of my trial begins.
Bishop Cauchon gathers
assessors like troops to his side.

I thought that the English captains
Talbot and Fastolf were my fiercest enemies,
but the bishop and his prosecutor d'Estivet
look to be more insidious and dangerous foes.
They wear robes of respectability and godliness,
and yet possess the teeth of wolves.

Most of my assessors
are drawn from the University of Paris
and are Dominican scholars.
Some came of their own free will,
others to curry English favor,
and the rest because they dared not refuse.
I pity their souls that they must

sit in judgment of God's will,
which must surely be a sin.

The bishop sends spies to gather
information about my past.
They fan the country
from Domrémy to Poitiers,
from Orléans to Patay to Reims,
casting a net over France,
hoping to snare something succulent
about me.
But the lures come back clean.

Cauchon chastises his men
for being bad soldiers.
They were not to find out the truth
about the girl who calls herself La Pucelle.
They were told to catch me
in some corruption,
to discover something
to defame my character.

Now the bishop
will be forced to improvise.

ON THE WAY TO COURT

A reverend assigned by Cauchon
named Jean Massieu
escorts me to the courtroom
for my first public session.

My hands chained
and my legs in irons,
I limp along the path.
The sky is one great cloud.
Even without sun
the brightness feels as harsh
as a deafening shriek.
I shield my eyes.

But I am outside
after a month of smelling
only my cell, my soiled clothes,
the filthy guards, and the latrine.
The air tastes crisp and frosty.
Snow lights upon the grass.

It is all so beautiful, I weep
and cannot move forward.

Reverend Massieu is touched by this
but kindly reminds me,
"Madame, I must deliver you to court."

One clang rings out alone,
but quickly is joined
by what sounds like a thousand others.
I have heard the church bells
from inside my cell
but they sound so much softer inside,
like a smattering of chimes in the wind.
This sounds like the proclamation
of God come to earth.

I feel the music tremble in my toes
and quiver my hands.
I could dance
were I not weighed down by chains.

I stand at the foot
of the Rouen cathedral.
It casts the shadow of a mountain
on the ground.
Nothing around, not river,
not flora, not beast—nothing
except the sky of heaven

matches its glory.
I fall to my knees.

I beg Reverend Massieu
to please let me stop
in the cathedral and hear mass,
to allow me to take communion
and confess my sins.

He shakes his head.
He is strictly forbidden
to allow me to do that.
I cannot enter the church
because I wear male clothes.

I might argue with him,
but he looks heartbroken
to deny me already.
Instead I ask if I might
simply kneel outside
the church door and pray.

He supposes there is no
harm in praying,
but he entreats me to be quick.
Soon I must be in court.

FIRST PUBLIC SESSION
February 21, 1431

I am summoned into the room
just as the bells sound eight times.

They provide me a bench
to sit on while questioned,
but I am never unfettered.
Should I tremble,
the metal will clatter and clank
and the sound of my fear
will be heard by all.

The courtroom appears to be carved
from one smooth stone.
Nested inside the Rouen Castle,
the room is smaller than I imagined
and crammed to capacity
with robed men.

Light floods the space
from windows above,
like a dozen birds' eyes
sent to watch over all.
When I look up,
the eaves and arches
appear to frown down on me,
intoning disapproval,
just like the voice
of the lead prosecutor, Jean d'Estivet.

"Unburden your conscience, Jehanne,"
d'Estivet says with heavy condescension.
"Touch the holy gospels
and take an oath to tell the truth
concerning all matters about which
we will question you."

He thrusts his Bible at me.

I WILL NOT SWEAR

I breathe deeply,
then look directly into his beady eyes.
"Perhaps you will ask me
things I cannot tell you."

The courtroom whirls
in immediate uproar.
Papers shuffle, priests mumble,
the public bystanders are agog.
No one expected me to refuse
to take d'Estivet's "simple" oath.

I explain that I will
gladly tell the court
about my parents
and where I come from
and all I have done on my journey
away from home.
But I cannot reveal exactly

what God has shared with me,
even if they threaten to cut off my head.

Cleric after cleric
beseeches me to take the oath—
some kindly, some sternly, some timidly,
some with the luster of a king.
But my answer never changes:
No.

Like starving men who suffer with scraps
though they really want and require a meal,
the group of robed clerics
finally swallows and accepts my offer.

The clergymen proceed to ask
a series of informational, boring questions.

Finally, they look to trick me.
The twisty-faced prosecutor
asks me to recite the *Paternoster*.

I know it is believed
that a witch cannot say
the Lord's Prayer aloud.

I pray the *Paternoster*
many times each day,
but I fear if I were to recite
the Lord's Prayer aloud here and now,
it would be very easy
for them to say I misspoke,
even if I did not.

I quiet my mind
and allow the solution
to be made clear. I smile.
"I will not say the Our Father
unless you hear my confession,
and then I will gladly say it."

Everyone in this room is aware
that whatever I say in confession,
right or wrong, good or bad,
cannot be repeated.

First bear trap averted.
I take a deep breath.

The clerics can tolerate
no more on the first day.
They dismiss me with heavy sighs.

AFTER DAY ONE

My cell appears more grim
and dark after I have walked
in the light of a cloudy day.
And it smells worse than I remember,
like someone vomited beside my pallet.

I pray that the movement
from this flea-ridden prison
to the ink-and-ledger courtroom
will not tangle my mind
like unspooled thread.
I hope to battle with words
as well as I fought
using cannons and swords.
I must avoid the *chausse-trappes*
the priests toss before my feet.

But what if by my words
I condemn myself?
Perhaps it would be

better, safer
to say nothing,
as I have been taught is proper
for those of my sex.

I beg God to help me
always know
the right thing to do
and say.

SECOND SESSION, SECOND STRENGTH
February 22, 1431

Something happens
when I step into the courtroom.
I shed the weariness of captivity,
lose the fear of a fiery stake.
My head clears
and my voice grows strong.

I forget that as a girl
I was taught to be silent.
I know in my heart
that in the eyes of God
I am equal to these robed men.
So I speak with the same authority
and assurance they do.

When the assessors cluck at me
to again swear their oath,
I shrug and refuse.

Impatient and unruly,
several clerics stitch one question quickly
on top of the next so that I do not know
what thread to follow,
what answer to give.
I cannot tell if they are trying
to confuse me
or just confusing themselves.

D'Estivet, the lead prosecutor,
tries to regain control and bellows,
"What kind of revelations
and apparitions did your king have?"

"I will not tell you this.
But send to the king
and he will tell you."

The day stealthily creeps into darkness
like a hand blocking out light
one finger at a time.
I do not even realize night has fallen
until everything turns black.

MY DAY OFF

I eavesdrop on my guards.
I pretend that I sleep
or that I cannot understand
what they say,
even though I have been living
among them for two months now.

The men merely repeat
what happened in court yesterday,
and quite inaccurately at that.
I try not to laugh
at the Englishmen's mangling
of French towns and names.

My mother always said
it was impossible to fool me
or win a disagreement,
because I can remember
the number of clouds
in the sky on any given day.

My memory is so skilled
and my wit as sharp
as an arrowhead.
I suppose the one consolation
of this trial
is that for once
I am not only able,
but encouraged,
to speak my mind.

MORE PRESSURE TO SWEAR
February 24, 1431

Instead of swearing their oath,
I swear that in the end
this court will not know how to condemn me
except by using the laws of the English.

The room shakes with fury at my words.
The clerics stomp and twist
as if I have set fire to their robes.

Bishop Cauchon bangs his gavel.
"Swear the oath or we could convict you
here and now for lying to us."

The bishop is a snake hiding in the grass.
He has been biding his time with this threat,
holding back his poisonous tongue.
But still, I refuse to be struck down.

The lead prosecutor, D'Estivet,
paces before me like a pendulum
and inquires if I know whether
I am in the grace of God.

I pause and think before I answer.
D'Estivet is clever, for only God
can put one in a state of grace.
If I answer yes,
I would be claiming
that all my sins have been forgiven
and I am with God, which I am not.
But if I answer no,
then I admit that I am in a state of sin,
which is what he wants me to say,
for then he will have grounds
to condemn me.
I take a deep breath.
"If I am not in a state of grace,
may God put me there.
If I am, may God keep me there."

After thirteen hours in the courtroom,
d'Estivet closes the day
by asking why I refuse to wear a dress.

The moment I arrived in Rouen,
I asked to be looked after by women
and would have burned my doublet.

I would like nothing more
than freshly laundered clothes,
not the flea-bitten, filthy rags itching my legs.
But how will I survive
unmolested in my cell in a dress?

If he gives me a dress,
I promise to leave the courtroom
and never return
and never again wear men's clothing.
Otherwise I must keep
the clothes I wear.

"Impossible,"
d'Estivet grumbles under his breath.

AM I A LADY WITHOUT A DRESS?

I wear men's clothing
because God commands it.
I wear trousers and tunic
to protect me from rape and abuse.
I first assumed male attire to travel
from my village to the city of Chinon
undetected in the night.
In trousers, I could ride free and steady
with a horse between my legs.
After the king granted me an army,
he suited me in armor, not a gown,
so I would be safe on the battlefield
and resemble the knights I would lead.
For no one in a dress, not even a queen,
rules or commands soldiers in France.
Respect is given to those who wear pants.
Authority and decisions are not granted
to the bejeweled and corseted.
Queens birth princes.
They do not govern.

God desired a maid at the helm
of the French army,
but I had to cut off my hair
and lose my dress.
I had to renounce my womanhood.

And yet,
underneath my steel
and chain mail,
underneath my trousers,
I am a lady, not a man.
And I believe
it is because of this
more than anything else
that they want me to burn.

ASK BETTER QUESTIONS
February 27, 1431

At first I thought that
these men of cloth
were just thick-skulled,
asking me day after day
to swear an oath
I told them clearly
I cannot and will not.
But now I see their aim.
They think if they whip at my ankles
until I am raw to the bone
and can bear no more,
I will do what they want.
What they do not know
is that I can withstand great pain.

A fly buzzes past my ear,
and for once I can hear
the subtly of its hum.
Usually there is so much noise
and distraction,

I cannot understand the question
I am being asked.

"You had both a banner and a sword
at Orléans and on the battlefield.
Which did you prefer, the banner
or the sword?"

I envision my standard in all its glory,
flapping like a crisp linen sheet
on a clothesline.
I have always been forty times fonder
of my banner than my sword.
I carried the banner when I attacked
enemies to avoid killing anyone.
And I never killed anyone on the battlefield
or anywhere else because of it.

SELF-CONFESSION

A dark cell offers
even more time for reflection
than I had while tending
my father's sheep.

I find that lately I miss my family
like one who has lost sight
misses color and shape;
like I never imagined I would.
I longed for glory,
to be more than Jehanne of Domrémy.
But sometimes when weariness,
doubt, and darkness
gnaw at my toes,
I wish someone else
had been chosen to be La Pucelle.

Tears splatter my tunic
like rain dinning a somber song,
and I confess that I am selfish
and do not want to die.

THE STRENGTH OF CATHERINE

I remember a time
our cow kicked my sister
halfway across the barn
when she was first learning to milk.
But the next day
Catherine returned to the stool,
bruised but not defeated,
and my mother taught her
to handle our bovine with care.

If my older sister
was ever afraid,
she hid her trepidation
as night hides the sun.

I often cried
when I burned the bread
or forgot kindling in the rain.
I lamented mistakes,
both major and minor,

as if my failures
were the greatest tragedies
in the world.

But Catherine
always faced tribulations
as if they were blessings, not sins.

A PREDICTION

March 1, 1431

As I have done every day
on my way to the courtroom,
I stop at the chapel
and pray in the doorway.
It gives me courage
for whatever the day holds.

The courtroom squirms and murmurs
as d'Estivet shuffles through his papers.
The scribes must spend all night
writing out the transcripts for him to consult,
and still he does not know what next to say.

A light winks
through the bird's-eye windows,
casting circles on the floor,
almost as if God signals me.
So I share a prediction with the courtroom:
before seven years have passed,
the English will suffer a greater loss

than they have ever suffered in France
through a great victory
that God will give the French.

D'Estivet drops his quill, quite stunned.
"When exactly will this happen?"

To this I say nothing.

"What year will it happen?"

I shake my head.

D'Estivet frowns, then clears his throat.
"What sign from God did you give your king?"

I want to stomp my foot, but I resist.
I repeat that I told him
I would not speak to the court
about matters meant for the king.
It does not concern this trial.

The lead prosecutor demands
that the clerics determine whether legally
I must answer this question.
The assessors huddle together
as if they shield each other from the cold.
They separate to two sides
and use their texts and notes to debate.

Back and forth, each side knocks down
the other like trees being felled.
After thirty minutes of deliberation,
they conclude that this question
does, indeed, concern my trial,
and I must answer it.

But I cannot tell them without perjury
what I have promised to keep secret.

D'Estivet tries to extract
more information about the king
and God's sign for Charles.

I answer as briefly as possible
until night releases me
from the courtroom
like a cell door being unlocked.

WHAT I AM GOING TO DO
WHEN I GET OUT OF HERE

Soak in a tub
and scrub until my skin
is red with purity.

Gallop through the woods
on my destrier,
the wind rushing in my ears.

Retrieve my banner
or if it be lost, have a new one sewn.

Be fitted for noble clothes
of the finest velvet, silks, and fur,
and have made a lady's blue gown
for court.

Buy back the Duke of Orléans,
for I know the treachery
that is imprisonment.

Kiss my sovereign's ring
and pledge my loyalty
like a newborn colt
kneeling at its mother's feet.

Purchase armor
to protect me
like a wall of steel.

Pray for my enemies.
Forgive them
for their injustice
and my imprisonment.

Run until I cannot breathe,
my arms outstretched,
my tongue catching rain.

Visit my mother and father
and show them the respect
they deserve.

Capture the Duke of Burgundy
and make him pledge loyalty
to King Charles VII.

Drive the English from France,
never to return.

Learn to read,
that I may never be deceived
by one more learned than me.
And so I can wage war
by both sword *and* pen.

SIXTH QUESTIONING IN PUBLIC
March 3, 1431

I hope the tremendous scroll
d'Estivet unfurls is no indication
of the number of questions
he intends to ask me today.

I feel slightly dizzy and grasp tightly
to my bench to steady myself.
Something rings inside my head
like a high-pitched screech.
Words whir past me,
and I imagine banners and pennons
swirling round my head.

Today's questioning bounces haphazardly
from one subject to the next,
so I can draw no line as to the meaning
the assessors wish to find.

Finally, d'Estivet asks me,
"How long were you in the tower
in Jean de Luxembourg's keep?"

I shake my head at his blatant attempt
to strangle me with my words.
He cares not how long I was in that tower
but wants to say I tried to kill myself
in leaping from it.
I explain to the court
that I was furious that the English
were coming to seize me.
My voice forbade me
to leap from the tower,
but I disobeyed
because I so feared the English.

"Did you say you would rather die
than fall into the hands of the English?"

I correct him.
I said I would rather
deliver my soul to God
than fall into English hands.

"Did you blaspheme the name of God?"

I take a long sip of water.
Everyone who has met me
knows I never use foul language
and have never cursed God.

With that d'Estivet indicates
for the guard to remove me from court.
He does not say we will reconvene tomorrow.

Is he finished with my inquiry?
Will this trial be shorter
than the assessment in Poitiers?

ONE LAST NIGHT

"Come, Jehanne,"
my escort, Jean Massieu, says kindly.
"There was hardly a cloud all day,
so the stars will crowd the sky tonight."

I ask Reverend Massieu
if we are done with the trial.

The reverend cannot meet my eyes.
He heard something
that he fears will bring me sadness.
Over the midday break,
Reverend Massieu heard the bishop
discuss moving questioning
to my prison chamber.

I will be deprived of the joy
and relief of leaving my cell.
Tears branch down my face.

"Reverend Massieu,
why do they hate me so?"

"You have shamed
and humiliated them.
You defeated their armies.
You are an illiterate girl
whom God speaks to
instead of them,
all learned men of the church.
They expect to tell you what to do,
not be instructed by you.
They fear you.
You are dangerous.
They must destroy you."

IS REVEREND MASSIEU MY FRIEND?

Jean Massieu is younger
than many of the other clerics.
I imagine if he had grown up
in Domrémy, he might have been
friends with my eldest brother, Jacquemin.
Nearly the same age,
they both possess the temperament
of good shepherds.

But Reverend Massieu was born Burgundian.
So even if he believes me innocent,
he must fight like a strong gale against me.
To contradict Bishop Cauchon
would jeopardize his position.
He could lose everything.

Nevertheless, the reverend treats me
with the kindness he would show
one of his parishioners.
He puts his robe at risk

and allows me to tiptoe
on the line of disobedience.
He prays for me.

He is my only friend
in Rouen.
And still
he is my enemy.

WHERE IS MY BROTHERHOOD?

Jean de Metz, La Hire,
and the Duke of Alençon
all vowed they would take an arrow
for me, yet where are they now?

Did their valiant words
and oaths extend no further
than the length of their swords?
Perhaps their allegiance
was confined to the battlefield.

I wonder if I was ever truly part
of the brotherhood of knights.

Or has La Pucelle
always been on her own?

BARRAGE OF QUESTIONS
March 10, 1431

Six assessors arrive midmorning
to my prison cell.
They must squeeze into my chamber,
and thus expel the three English guards
to make room for their table and chairs,
Bibles, ink, and papers.

Today they ask about my capture.

Did you spend many days
in Compiègne?

Did your voice tell you
that you would be captured
when you were approaching Compiègne?

Did you have a shield and arms
when you were captured?

Did you have a horse
when you were captured?

Who gave you a horse?

Did the king ever give you other riches?

Would you have gone if your voice
ordered you to attack Compiègne
but signified that you would be taken
captive?

That is a good question.
Yes, I would.
And yes, I did.

SUCCESS OR FAILURE?

What I have accomplished
through God's will
is beyond any ambition
I ever conceived for myself.

How could I imagine
I would lead an army of men
and crown the king of France?

Still, I thought I was the warrior
God intended to deliver France
from her enemies.

I believed that because
I followed divine orders,
I would never fail.

Somewhere along the path
I must have stepped
beyond God's plan.

Why else would I
fall into English hands?

Or has that always been my fate?

I am no longer sure
whether I have succeeded
or failed in my mission.
I suppose only time will tell.

A CREEP OF CLERICS
March 12, 1431

It is earlier than yesterday
when the Burgundian churchmen
enter my cell this morning.
I have just returned from the latrine.

Some of the inquisitors
have changed, although
it is rather hard to tell.
Robed clerics and masters of theology
look very similar.
With slumped shoulders
and squatty frames,
many of them shuffle around
with no sense of urgency,
slow as a bale of turtles.
They even look a bit like turtles
with their wrinkled necks
and heavy eyelids.

I have one time or another
been asked all their questions already.
The days and my responses
are beginning to meld
into a sludge of sameness.
But perhaps that is the point—
to question me until I contradict myself,
to conduct the examination
in my cell, not the courtroom,
so I have no place to retreat.
In essence, they want to break me down.

Three hours of inquiry this morning
focused on my male attire.
Who exactly does
my wearing hosen harm,
except perhaps it hinders
the ruffian guards who wish to rape me?

Who says I am a daughter of God
only if I wear a dress?
God does not.
These turtles wear robes.
Are robes so unlike dresses?
Men of the church wear garments
that wrap around them
like ill-fitting peasant gowns
and nobody accuses them of heresy.

TIRED AND BORED

My eyelids sag
heavy as the chains at my feet.
Exhaustion becomes
a cough rusted in my throat,
a dull pain cinching my gut.

For the last two weeks,
as soon as I drift into dream,
the guards holler
and bang their swords
to shake me from slumber.
Even if I scream and protest,
they persist in their torment.

Even more miserable—
beyond sleeping
there is nothing to do
in this cell.
I have counted the bricks,
memorized the number

of links in my chain,
recited every prayer I know.
To relieve the tedium
I even resorted to singing
with my voice of a horse.
The guards swiftly threatened
to cut out my tongue.

I have never relished idleness.
On the farm, work never ceased.
And battle is preparation
followed by action.

I almost look forward
to the clerics visiting my cell.
I prefer questioning to silence.

At least I have something
to do.

BREAKING DOWN AND GIVING IN

March 13, 1431

A cleric of more significance
named Brother Jean Le Maistre
accompanies Bishop Cauchon
and participates in my interrogation.

Like a child who will do anything
to attract his parents' attention,
including jumping up and down
and howling like a beast,
Bishop Cauchon tries hard to impress
Brother Jean Le Maistre.

Cauchon and Le Maistre are keen
to discuss the sign I gave to my king.
Weary of this question,
I give in and tell them the sign
was an angel bringing a gold crown
to King Charles and assuring the king
that through my labors
and with the help of God,

the kingdom of France
would be restored to him.

"Why did God send you
and not someone else
a sign for your king?"

How do they expect me to know this?
It must have pleased God
to drive back the king's enemies
through a simple maid.
My throat feels like someone
has fed me dirt.
"Might I have some water?"

"When we are finished with our questions
you can have water," Cauchon tells me.
He then says to his secretary,
"Do not record that last part
in today's transcript."

Jean Le Maistre turns his head side to side,
examining my cell for mandrakes and potions,
then sniffs the air with a foul expression.
He asks me, "Did the crown have a pleasing smell?"

I have no memory of this.
I try to swallow saliva to relieve
the pain of my scratchy throat.

"Did you go to Paris
because you were counseled
to do so by your voice?"

"No, I went at the request of nobles
who wanted to make an assault."
My voice sounds as parched
as a field gone months without rain.
Still I am not given water.

"Did you have a revelation
that you would be captured?"

At this point my voice
is the crunchy whisper of an old hag.
"After I had a revelation
that I would be captured, I turned over
most of the conduct of war to the captains.
But I did not tell the captains
I would be captured."

The clerics seem satisfied for the day
and do not return in the afternoon.

I am not given water
until my evening meal.

STAY STRONG AND REMEMBER YOUR PURPOSE

I recall a day
not long after I first heard God's voice.
I had finished my field work
and before the midday bells,
before the sun reached its summit,
I waded far into the meadow.
I was like a shipwrecked sailor,
so deeply alone
no person could hear me
if I sang or screamed.

I felt scared and incapable
of my calling.
Tears streamed from my eyes
as if they might never end.

I tried to empty my mind
of the world.
I knelt and waited
to hear God's voice.

The field's absolute stillness
shuddered through my bones.
Above me clouds gathered
like a simmering stew.
I cried aloud,
"Why me?
I am no one.
Maybe You want
one of my brothers instead?"

The caw of a bird,
a great rustle of wind
and the sky shone brilliant
like the clouds were made of sun,
and God said:
It is you I call, Jehanne.

I understood in that moment
that no matter what I had been taught
or seen or thought I knew,
a girl could and would save France.

REPETITION

March 14, 1431

No hesitancy today,
but right to my examination.
The clerics seem as eager to attack
me with questions
as a butcher is to slaughter
his fattened calf on Martinmas.

Why did you leap from
the tower at Beaurevoir?

When you leaped, did you believe
you were killing yourself,
which is a mortal sin?

Two or three days after your leap,
did you curse or deny God?

We have evidence that you cursed God.
Would you like to refer to it?

I shake my head.
Why would I listen
to the words of my captors
or these men intent on my guilt?

Enduring day after day of interrogation,
I grow as tired as an old woman
who must carry all her wares on her back.
Even though some of these questions are new,
I want to avoid being asked the same things
should my trial be moved to Paris,
as is rumored might happen next.
I ask if I may have a copy
of these questions and my answers
to give to my next examiners.
Perhaps all this repetition can be avoided.

SEEING FLAMES

There has been no direct mention
of fire during my hearing.
Even my guards
have stopped tormenting me
with talk about a stake
in the courtyard,
about how the flames
melt flesh before one burns.

But my dreams
are not unburdened.
I swear that I not only
see the flames,
I feel the sharp knife
of their heat.
So severe are my night terrors
that I sleep like one
with a fatal fever.
I scream out for help,
scream out for release.

I wake to find
it was just another dream.
But I do not feel safe or secure.
The flames feel too close,
as if they circle my bed,
licking my body,
ready to consume me
like the jowls of a hungry bear.

SPEECH AND SILENCE

For the greater part of my life,
I feared that if I opened my mouth
I might unleash a fire
I would not be able to control.

Trapped in a tower of silence,
I believed the thoughts in my head
would cause me harm
and disapproval.

All that I say in court
is being recorded for posterity.
I know that speaking the truth
may lead to my condemnation,
but I will not be silent
out of fear.

I hope and pray
for God to save me,
to free me from my captivity.

But perhaps I am not
the one meant to be saved.
Maybe my mission
is not yet complete.
Perhaps instead of saving France
I am meant to save something
or someone else.

VERIFICATION

March 24, 1431

Today follows
a new protocol.
I am read all the questions
I have been asked
and my answers to them.
They want me to confirm
that the record they have kept
reflects what I actually said,
and they seek my verification
of my words.

I find corrections need be made
only thrice, and the issues
are of minor consequence.
The scribe is quite capable.

I take heart in this.
I ask the man who escorted
me to the courtroom,
Reverend Jean Massieu,

if this means
the trial is finally
coming to a conclusion.

"No, La Pucelle.
On the contrary,
it is just about to begin."

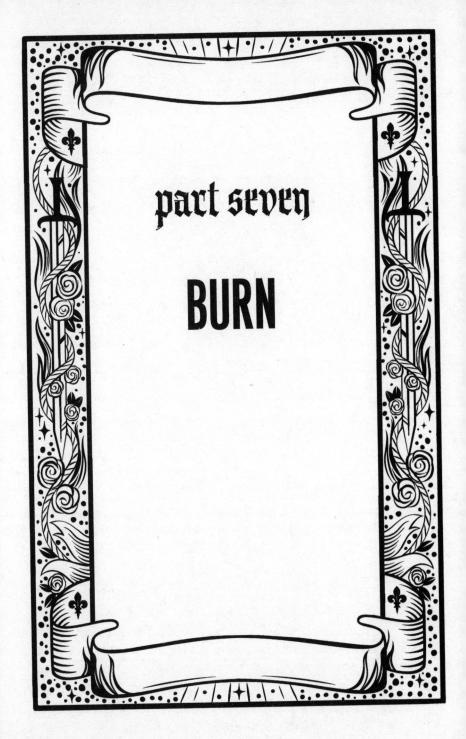

part seven

BURN

ORDINARY TRIAL
March 27, 1431

I thought I might
never again see the sky,
that I might be confined
to my cell evermore,
but this morning
Jean Massieu escorts me
down the corridor
and outside to Rouen Castle.

It smells like spring,
like budding leaves and grass.
The sky croaks with morning birds
busily gathering twigs and straw
for their nests.
I pretend it requires great effort
to haul my chains
so that I can linger
extra moments in the sun.

Inside the castle's great chamber,
the robed men stare at me
with faces as serious as the pox.

Jean d'Estivet, the prosecutor,
reads a petition to me in French
which declares that I must answer
all questions regarding my trial
or face excommunication from the church.
If excommunicated,
I would then be handed over to the state.

D'Estivet clears his throat
with a prolonged cough.
"The men gathered here
are learned churchmen
who seek not revenge
or corporal punishment,
but your return to the path
of truth and salvation."

SEVENTY ARTICLES

The prosecutor stands to accuse me
of seventy articles of crimes
against the church.
Some of these articles
contain numerous accounts
of my indiscretions and sins.

By midday break
I weary from the sound
of quills scraping across parchment
as the secretaries mark down
my every response.

The robed crows
clearly wish to peck out my eyes,
not save me from myself.
But I remain firm.
Let them prod and strike
and enumerate their articles.
I cannot be blinded

from the light of God.
I will serve up the righteous truth
with or without eyes.

By evening
at least half the men gathered
have nodded off
during some point in the proceedings,
for nothing new is revealed.
D'Estivet accuses me.
Then over and again
I reject the accusation.
I claim innocence
seventy separate times.

EASTER

No one talks of my death,
but I feel it in the room
creeping toward me
like a poisonous fog.
The walls of my cell
close in on me today,
as if I will soon be snuffed out.

It is a day to rejoice,
the day Christ is risen
from the dead.
I wonder if my parents celebrate.
Do they know how I suffer?
Can they find peace
with their daughter behind bars,
pleading for her innocence,
for her life?

I hope the king enjoys this Easter,
feasts in the light of the Lord
for both of us.
I hope he thanks God for his freedom.
I hope he sheds no tears
for La Pucelle.
I cry plenty enough for myself.

I want to be jubilant,
to chirp with the birds
and praise this life.
This may be my final Easter,
my nineteenth year.

I am not ready to die
but want to live fully.
I want to praise God in church
and on the battlefield,
to praise God in all that I do.

I clasp my hands
and pray that God deliver me
from this cell.
I thank Him for his mercy
and trust that He knows best
what shall become of me.

REDUCTION

April 5, 1431

My long list of crimes
and sins against man and church
shrink like steamed spinach

from seventy to
twelve. The articles are read
aloud in legal

language. Dressed up to
sound fair and factual as
two plus two equals

four. But this trial
is no simple equation,
and the priests know it.

THE ESSENCE OF THE ARTICLES: 1-6

One:
When I was thirteen
I first heard the call of God
in my father's garden
among the onions and daisies
and it frightened and disoriented me
like a boulder had dropped on my head.
But because I came to understand my mission,
followed words in the clouds and my heart
that these learned men could not hear,
and because I will submit myself
to the scrutiny of God alone,
these churchmen on earth say I have sinned.

Two:
In Chinon appeared, like the star of Bethlehem,
a gold crown to prove to King Charles
that I am La Pucelle sent by God.
These men in robes did not see

the crown with their own eyes,
so they accuse me of lying.

Three:
Why would God choose
to speak to a lowly peasant girl?
If I knew this answer,
would I not be divine myself?
There are mysteries that God
alone understands,
but these learned men fail
to comprehend that,
or perhaps they just cannot accept
that God speaks to a girl.

Four:
I have accomplished many feats
through revelation:
found a sword buried beneath an altar,
recognized King Charles
without knowing his face.
Like a prophet,
I have been given foreknowledge,
but instead of seeing this as heaven-sent,
it must be my invention
or the devil's.
I am called a witch.

Five:
Women must look like women
and men alone be attired like men.
Women must behave like women
and only men act valiant and fierce,
despite whatever gifts God grants you.
In fact, the more I have accomplished,
the more I am despised.

Six:
I used a code to signal my commanders.
The sign of the cross
indicated to do the opposite
of what my letter proposed.
Cleverness in a woman
must be crushed and punished.
It cannot come from God.

THE ESSENCE OF THE ARTICLES: 7-12

Seven:
Thou shalt not disobey thy parents.
I left home to embark
on my mission against their will.
I am a disrespectful and bad daughter.
I am my parents' only living daughter.
It stings like salt on a wound
to hear the clerics say I care not
for my family, when I love no one
but God, and perhaps King Charles,
more.

Eight:
I threw myself from the tower.
I will never convince them
that it was an attempt
to escape,
not from this world,
but from captivity.

Men who have not been prisoners
cannot understand.

Nine:
I have remained a virgin
to the great fury
of nearly every man I have met,
because there is power
in not becoming a mother or wife.
It makes me more equal to a man.
I promised God to remain pure.
God knows I committed no mortal sins,
or He would abandon me to suffer alone.
And He does not abandon me.
This boils the britches of Bishop Cauchon.

Ten:
I love God and King Charles
above others, but who does not?

Eleven:
I believe in God the Almighty,
creator of heaven and earth,
and worship no other.
I have pledged my loyalty
to no demon or false god.
I know it was God who spoke to me,
or I would never have left my village.
No one would embark

on such an improbable mission,
and certainly not a seventeen-year-old girl.

Twelve:
I listen first to my voice,
for it is God,
and second to the teachings
of the robed men on earth.
The first is direct divinity,
the second an interpretation.

PRETENSE

Like chefs arguing
over how to season stew,
the clerics debate

the twelve articles.
They act as if their judgment
remains in question,

when my trial is
as predetermined as day
turning into night.

But no one dares to
speak about how I shall pay
for my heinous crimes.

They gather tinder
but refrain from igniting
a stake with flames yet.

RECURRENT DREAM

I am burning again,
but this time
I am not in my father's barn.
Bound to a wooden stake,
wishing for the smoke
to fill my nostrils
and choke off my breath,
I swear I feel the singe
of every flame,
hotter than boiling oil,
sharper than a sword.
I smell my acrid hair catch fire,
scream as my fingernails melt
into my flesh.

Around my crackling scaffold,
shouts from the crowd
ring out like enemy battle cries.
I scream *"Jesu! Jesu!"*
but when I look to heaven,

forks of flame
blind my eyes.

There is no escape for me,
only an end.
There is no freedom for me,
only death.
And it takes so long
to burn away a life—
minutes upon minutes
I must stand in fire,
one for every year
I have drawn air.

BAD FISH
April 18, 1431

I fear I am dying.
I cannot hold down anything
and move from sweats to shivers
with the ferocity of a raging storm.
Over a week now I have been teetering
between consciousness and madness.

They fed me bad fish.
I should not have eaten it,
but it was a gift from the bishop
to celebrate Easter.

Today more than half
a dozen men enter my prison cell,
one of whom is Bishop Cauchon,
and another is a doctor
called on to attend me.

I must look like a ghost
because all the men
stare at me with the gravity
of leaden boots.

I hear the bishop whisper
to the doctor,
"She must be kept alive at all costs."

Strange that these men
who threaten me with excommunication
and soon enough a burning stake
fear losing me to a natural cause.
I thought the bishop had poisoned me,
but that must not have been the case.

The men tell me they have come
in love and friendship
to comfort and encourage me.
Am I dreaming?

The bishop softens his tone.
"You have been questioned
on great and difficult matters.
Many of the things you confessed
are a danger to the faith."
This man who has thus far shown me
no love grasps my fevered hand.

"As you are an ignorant, unlearned woman,
we offer you kind counsel for the salvation
of your body and soul."

I blink my eyes, then dry-retch
into the bucket beside my bed.
"I believe that I am dying of illness.
May I please be allowed confession
and the Eucharist?"

"Only if you confess and submit to the church
can we administer the sacraments to you,"
Bishop Cauchon says with a strange smile.

My head swirls,
and I dizzy opening my eyes.
My voice breaks like tiny twig.
"Please."

"Will you submit to the church?"
the bishop demands of me again.

My words are so soft and stumbling
the bishop must lean close to hear them.
He repeats what I say to the others in my cell.
"She says she loves God and serves Him.
She is a good Christian.

But she cannot submit
in the way that we wish."

Bishop Cauchon drops my hand
and steps away from the bed.
"Foolish child, do you not wish
for the church to save your soul?"

I am so weary now,
I can do nothing more
than close my eyes.

REPENT

May 2, 1431

After two weeks
I recover from my illness,
but it has weakened me.
Like a man
who has broken his back,
I will never walk easily again.

When I enter the courtroom today,
I cough and gasp from the stench
of stale old men.

An ancient theologian named
Master Jean de Châtillon awaits me.
His neck slouches into his shoulders,
making him look like a storm-ravaged rock.

He explains in a gravelly voice,
"You must submit to the church, not God alone.
If you persist in your belief

that you have authority outside of the church,
you will be considered a heretic."

I remain silent and unmoving as a frozen pond.

The master pushes his glasses
farther back on his nose.
"It is dangerous to lie
about things that extend to God."

The old man pauses
to give me time to consider his words.
I stare into Master Châtillon's steely eyes.

The old man waggles his finger at me
and demands that
I return to the path of truth!

Every head in the assembly
nods at his words.
Some of the robed clerics
plead with piteous eyes
for me to repent.

I explain that I believe
in the church on earth,
but as to what I say and do,
I leave that to God.

Châtillon barks out a final warning,
that if I do not submit to the church
I will be abandoned by the church.
Both my body and soul will face fire—
my soul eternal hellfire
and my body fire in this world.

If I saw the fire now,
I tell them, I still would not
change my words.

TORTURE

May 9, 1431

I heave my chains
up a winding staircase.
Little slits of sun
like clusters of stars
illuminate the path
to the castle's tower.

But I am not taken
up to the turret
to breathe fresh air
or take in the view.
I am dragged here
to be shown the rack
that separates joints and limbs,
sharp hooks, spikes, and hammers
designed to crush bones
and make people cry out
whatever their tormentors require of them,
whether or not it is the truth.
They want me to scream and thrash

when they hold a hot iron spike
up to my eye.
But I remain silent and still.

The holy men
warn me to tell the truth
about all that I denied in my trial,
or through torture I will
be led back to the path of righteousness.

I smile.
"If you tear my limbs apart
and separate my soul from my body,
I still will not tell you anything else.
And if I tell you anything,
later I will say that you
forced it out of me."

The robes huddle in debate.
One man fears
if they torture me, it may give
their whole case against me
less credence.
It may call into question
all they have done
right and well.

A different cleric lobbies
to torture the sorceress

and see if I do not admit
my lies and sins!

Bishop Cauchon eyes me
up and down.
"Do you understand
that you will be burned?"

I try to keep my voice steady
as I explain,
"I am afraid of your fire,
but I wait on God."

Cauchon sighs heavily.
"I fear the instruments of torture
would profit her little.
We will not apply them
at this time."

NEVER GOING HOME

If I close my eyes,
I can imagine Mother
mending Father's favorite scarf,
the one with the blue-and-brown fringe,
as she rocks beside the hearth.
She hums, her voice like a soft breeze,
and tends a burbling broth.

Father's heavy boots
announce his presence.
He kicks them soundly
against the front step
to shake off mud and manure
before entering the house.
Mother warns him to keep
his spoon out of her broth.
It is not properly seasoned yet.

Hauviette and my brother Jean
expect their first baby,

one I will never meet on earth.
Unfortunately, it will be a girl,
but the next child they feel certain
will be a little Jean.

Mother will treat her first and only
granddaughter as if she is
the queen of France.
Jacquemin and his wife have five sons,
but they live too far away to spoil.

Pierre refuses to trade his sword
for a pitchfork.
He continues to fight
for King Charles against the English.
Mother's tears dampen her pillow
with great fear that Pierre will never
return home.

And as if Catherine and I
are ships swallowed by the sea,
my parents mourn
the loss of both their daughters
until their final breaths.

ABJURATION
May 24, 1431

The bishop designs a spectacle
to terrify me into submission.

Entombed by hundreds of armed men,
I am led past the marketplace,
where a stake on which
I will be consumed by fire
has been erected.
My knees slacken
and I stumble before it.
I forget how to draw breath.
I close my eyes, but the stake
burns in my brain.

The streets crowd
as they did the day I arrived in Rouen.
People snicker, spit, and chant,
"Burn the witch!"

They drag me to the cemetery
at the abbey of Saint-Ouen
where stand two scaffolds—
one for me,
the other for the clergy judges.

A theologian delivers a sermon
on my misdeeds, admonishes me,
and bids me one final time
to repent and submit to the church.
A piece of parchment
on which only a few lines are written
is shoved before my face,
and I am urged to sign it.

The crowd shouts and clamors
louder than soldiers midbattle.
Like I stand beside a firing cannon,
I cannot hear to think.
I wish my voice would
advise me what to do.

As I eye the tumbrel ready to wheel me
to my stake, one cleric says,
"If you sign the paper,
you will be turned over to the church.
Accept your woman's dress
as we request, or you will die."

I stare at the document.
If I am turned over to the church,
that means I will finally be sent
to a church prison,
provided I wear women's clothes
and sign the abjuration.
I grab the pen and mark an X
on the parchment.
Though I cannot read the paper,
I am told that by this action
I save myself.
All the clergy praise me.

But not the mob of English
and Burgundians.
The crowd boos and hisses,
"Death to the witch!"
They throw stones at my head.
The guards must restrain
the people by force.

I signed the paper
to release myself
from English prison,
but I do not in truth
submit to the church.
An X is not my signature.
I know well how to sign my name.

After examining my abjuration,
Bishop Cauchon tells me,
"You are now sentenced
to a penance of perpetual imprisonment.
You will eat only the bread of sorrow
and drink only the water of affliction."

I am escorted by armed guard
out of the courtyard.

But they return me
to my same English prison cell.

"I thought I was to be taken
to a church prison!" I cry.

My guards laugh
and throw women's clothes at me.

I change into my dress
and hand over my doublet.
Maybe now I will be delivered
to a church prison
and attended by nuns.

WHY I SIGNED THAT PAPER

I am tired of these
manacles around my ankles,
tired of the cold, the damp,
of the deepening dark.
I am weary of itching, of aches,
and my own foul smell.
I have grown sick of nasty men's trousers,
of the soldiers' fists and threats of rape.
I thought I would be moved to a church prison
when I signed their abjuration,
but I returned to the same cell.
They lied. They have always lied.

I thought I might escape death,
might find a way to escape a new prison
and return to the fresh air,
but I see now that will never be my fate.
I must die for my beliefs.

But the fire—
I still quake with fear.

Without a guiding voice,
my thoughts unravel.
I am constantly negotiating
a terrain of sight and blindness.

I feel so terribly alone.
I pray that God
steadies my nerves
and prepares my soul.
I pray He sends me courage,
because right now
I need to be filled with something
greater than fear.

RELAPSE

May 28, 1431

I wake to find
my dress has vanished.
In its place return
my sodden and smelly
men's apparel—
a tunic, a doublet, hose, and a short hood.
I sleep in only a sliver of a slip.
It would be quite improper
to leave my bed in it alone,
surrounded as I am by men.

Three English guards
observe me closely,
clearly interested
in what I will do.

"What happened
to the dress I have been wearing
the last several days?"

The tall guard chuckles
like I have said something amusing.
"Come here and I will whisper in your ear
what has become of your dress."

I have not visited the latrine
since yesterday afternoon
and am in need of it now.
I pick up the tunic.
If I put this on, I violate my oath
to never again wear men's clothes
and will be handed over to the English
and burned at the stake.
But I was supposed to be taken
to an ecclesiastical prison
and be guarded by nuns,
yet they left me to rot
in this English castle.
If they violated their side
of the agreement,
might I not breach mine?

I clasp my hands in prayer.
Please, God, tell me what to do.

Take up the tunic, Jehanne.
Do not fear the fire;
on the other side lies Paradise.

I rub the hose
between my fingers.
It feels rougher than I remember.

The guard with a mole on his cheek
pokes me in the arm.
"Why do you remain under those covers?
Are you hiding something?"
He yanks away my blanket,
then eyes me with violence and desire.
"Today I will make you a woman!"

I swiftly kick his leg,
and while he rubs where it smarts,
I pull on the hose,
lace them tighter than a corset
to protect myself.

"She has relapsed.
We must tell the bishop at once,"
the putrid-smelling guard says.

Without being summoned,
Bishop Cauchon and his secretary
appear in my cell,
as if they had been watching everything
through a hole in the wall.
"By taking up men's clothing,
you have sinned and failed

to honor the contract you signed.
You are a relapsed heretic.
You are excommunicated.
The church turns its back
on you, Jehanne La Pucelle.
You will be turned over
to secular authorities."

LAST SACRAMENTS

May 30, 1431

All the clerics agree
that I am a relapsed heretic,
but some wish to give me
a second chance to repent.
Others say they want to make
a plea to the English for leniency
so that I might not be put to death by fire.
But the men most in charge
just wish to turn me over
and let come what may.

The robed men
must feel some pang
of responsibility, and perhaps even guilt,
for sending an innocent to the flames,
because I am finally allowed
to make confession
and receive the Eucharist,
two sacraments

those who are excommunicated
are not supposed to be given.

I pray with Reverend Jean Massieu.
Tears well in his eyes
when I sob and confess
that I fear the fire
and beg God to forgive me
for signing the abjuration
and denying His voice.

To eat and drink of Christ's body
heals me more than any doctor or potion.
Even though no one else can see it,
the light of God radiates in my room.
It eases my fear
knowing that in my death
God will be beside me.

SAYING GOODBYE

When someone is sick,
death rattling the doorknob,
you sit bedside, cry,

pray, hold her hand, and
say *je t'aime*. Then release her
like a baby bird

to fly away. But
I must face fire without
friends or family.

At my end, I can
only imagine their smiles
like a soothing balm,

remember the smell
of my mother's hair, pretend
that I lean against

Pierre's strong shoulder.
We cannot gather like clouds
for grieving and tears.

Catherine waits for me.
I hear her calling my name.
Still I hate to leave

like a boat unmoored
in a vicious storm, without
saying my goodbyes.

THE FIRE

May 30, 1431

They shear off the little hair
left on my head.
Large sloppy tears cleanse my face.

I plead not to be removed from my cell.
"I should have been put in a church prison!
My death is your doing!"
I scream at Bishop Cauchon.

Cauchon denies responsibility.
He shoves a rough black tunic in my face
and forces me to wear a miter with the words
Heretic, Relapse, Apostate, Idolater.

It seems every armed soldier in Rouen
escorts me to the tumbrel.
This simple cart generally used to haul manure
will convey me to my death in the marketplace.

I roll slowly through
the angriest mob I have ever seen,
the poor and rich united
by their hate for me.
Ten thousand people
trample one another
to get an up-close
and final look at the French witch.

Four stages have been raised
in the square:
one for ecclesiastical judges
and notable people;
one for secular judges and the bailiff;
one for the clergyman who will
deliver to me a final sermon;
and the highest platform
for me and the stake
on which I will burn.

Cauchon reads me the placard
he erected before my stake:
"Jehanne who had herself
named La Pucelle is a liar,
pernicious person, abuser of people,
soothsayer, superstitious woman,
blasphemer of God, presumptuous,
unbeliever in the faith of Jesus Christ,

boaster, idolater, cruel, dissolute,
invoker of devils, apostate,
schismatic, and heretic."

After another robed man
preaches me a final sermon,
Bishop Cauchon yells,
"Jehanne, you are fallen again
into these errors and crimes
as the dog who returns to his vomit!
We separate and abandon you from the church
and give you over to secular power."
His words incite the crowd to cheers
and shoves and madness.

"Oh, Rouen, I am much afraid
that you may suffer for my death,"
I say as they chain me to my pyre.
"I pardon you for any harm
you have done to me."
I look around with terror
for anything that might comfort me.
"May I please be given a cross?"

Unexpectedly, a rough-looking
English soldier here to control the mob
ties two sticks of kindling into a cross
and hands it to me.

I kiss the cross that it may bring me
courage and peace,
then tuck it inside my robe.

I will not be strangled,
as are most people sentenced to die by fire.
They want me to smell my flesh cook.

A torch lights the bottom of the pyre.
Immediately I feel the heat,
smell the burning wood,
hear a crackling of tinder.

When the pain comes
like a thousand sharpened swords,
I cry out, *"Jesu! Jesu!"*
Tears boil on my face.
I try to see my way to heaven,
but smoke blurs my eyes.
"Jesu!" Please let me die quickly.

But I do not.
I endure twenty minutes
of unfathomable suffering.

After my screams subside
and the English are certain I am dead,
they rake back the fire
and raise up my naked body

to expose and dishonor me,
to prove to the world
that I was only a woman.

The flames are then relit
until they reduce my carcass to ash.

But none of this distresses me,
for I look down from Paradise now.

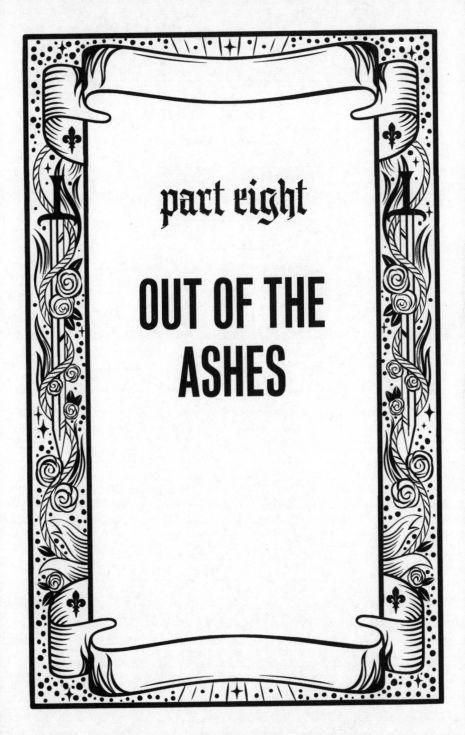

part eight

OUT OF THE
ASHES

AFTER THE FIRE

My heart was not consumed
by the flames
but lay in the blackened embers
to remind all present
that the English can burn my body,
but they will never destroy my spirit.
They dumped my ashes
unceremoniously into the Seine
so that no groups
might rise to protest my death
or worship the relics of my body.
So that I will be forgotten.

But twenty-five years after I died,
after the conflict
between France and England ceased
and the French were victorious,
my mother pledged on bended knees
to king and country
that her daughter was unfairly judged,

never sinned
but was an innocent put to the flame.
She said only my vindication could calm
her tormented soul.
My rehabilitation would also strengthen
the validity of King Charles,
as his triumph over the English
was due in large part
to my success on the battlefield.
And I helped to crown him king.

King Charles VII wanted
none of his reign to be tarnished
by association with someone infamous
and called for a reexamination of my trial.
He sent clergymen
to interview those who knew me best—
villagers in Domrémy,
citizens of Orléans and Poitiers,
the clergy yet alive who participated
in my original trial,
and many men who served
beside me in battle.

In July 1456,
I was officially exonerated
and the trial of condemnation
declared null and invalid.
A cross was erected

in the Old Marketplace in Rouen
to commemorate where I made
the ultimate sacrifice
and was burned alive
for my faith and good deeds.
The cross remains there
more than five hundred years later.

After many petitions and much debate,
in 1920, the Catholic Church
canonized me as a saint.
The same church
that condemned me centuries before
finally acknowledged that my works
were miraculous and of God.

My countrymen have praised me
in every generation as a national hero
and celebrate my death on May 30
each year with a festival and holiday.

I have risen from the ashes,
an angel on a holy white steed,
the most well-known girl
and warrior of my era.

My story has been translated
into thousands of languages.
The tale of a girl ahead of her time

who fearlessly led an army to victory,
the account of an illiterate farmer's daughter
who outwitted scholars,
who spoke her truth
and sacrificed her life,
has bridged cultures and centuries.

I understand now my final purpose—
through my words and deeds
to inspire others
to find hope and strength
to speak and act.

The girls who fear
the fire inside themselves,
I burned for them.

AUTHOR'S NOTE

I first became fascinated with Joan of Arc in fourth grade, when Sister Esther shared with my catechism class the story of a girl who was called by God to fight for her country. I was neither a tomboy nor particularly fascinated with war. I was not overly religious, but I felt an almost immediate kinship with someone who lived five and half centuries before me. I could not erase the image of a girl who burned at the stake for her beliefs, who was put to death for daring to be different. I too often felt awkward or like an outsider, a little different from even my friends. Like Joan, I was searching for a place where I would not only fit in, but shine. What struck me about Joan of Arc was that she was a girl who rose beyond her station. She refused to accept that she could be nothing more than a farmer's daughter. She believed in herself and her calling so strongly that she convinced others to follow her. She helped to save her nation. Somehow, against all odds, she achieved the impossible. And ultimately, she sacrificed her life for her beliefs. At nine years old, I could not imagine possessing such strength, but boy, did I want it. I still do. I have never lost my admiration for Joan. Decades later I dreamed of writing a book about her.

Along the way, I had to make decisions in the hope that the story will best be served by some deviation from the historical record. As much as possible I tried to stay true to the facts contained in Joan's trial transcripts and the interviews conducted with the people who knew her, but in a few cases I purposely altered things. Joan very clearly stated that she heard three distinct voices: the voices of Saint Michael, Saint Catherine, and Saint Margaret, not a singular voice from God. I chose to simplify three voices into one, not only for ease of reading and comprehension, but more importantly because although in the fifteenth century hearing the voices of saints was not hard for people to imagine, modern readers do not in large part pray to saints. However, many people pray to God or Allah or a higher being, perhaps even follow what they believe to be God's plan for them, or they have been driven at one time or another by an internal voice.

A second place where many of Joan's actions and feelings became more my invention than born out of fact was in Joan's childhood. It is generally accepted that Joan had three brothers and a sister and grew up in Domrémy, where her father acted as the dean, but otherwise knowledge of her youth is limited compared to all the information about the battles she fought and her trial and condemnation. Further, I created an internal struggle for Joan throughout her journey. The Joan of the historical record is largely pious and a brave warrior, but we do not know much of her beyond that. I wanted to emphasize in this book that Joan was of flesh and blood. Wherever possible I incorporated real dialogue from the transcripts and set scenes when and where they occurred, but some of the battles and days in court have been collapsed, combined, or omitted entirely. The first drafts of this book edged closer to nonfiction, but as I continued to rewrite, I made decisions so that Joan and her journey might come more alive on the page.

I love research and read as many biographies and histories of the period as I could get my hands on, several of which are listed in the bibliography should you wish to read further about Joan. One remarkable primary source available is the complete transcript for Joan's 1431 trial of condemnation and the interviews conducted for her exoneration in 1456. Joan has one of the most complete medieval trial records in existence, and the interviews about her provide some of the best insight as to what it was like to be a girl in fifteenth-century France. Joan is well known to posterity largely because such meticulous records of her case were kept by the Catholic Church.

I also had the good fortune to travel to France and visit the city of Rouen, where Joan spent the last portion of her life. Several of the buildings still standing in Rouen date back to the medieval period. The winding streets are narrow, and the city remains dominated by its location on the Seine. After wandering the town, I could imagine how Joan felt entering Rouen and as she walked to and from the courthouse. And to further experience what it was like in Joan of Arc's time, you can visit a 360-degree artist-rendered panorama of Rouen in 1431. The panorama, housed inside a dome, offers a bird's-eye view of the daily life of the period as day shifts into night, then rises to the dawn of a new morning. Eerie music adds an uneasy and otherworldly element in the background. In 2015, the Jeanne d'Arc Historial, an interactive museum about Joan of Arc, opened inside the Archbishop's Palace where Joan was sentenced in 1431 and exonerated in 1456. I stood in the courtroom where Joan was condemned and tried to imagine her bravery. In one room of the historial, flames encircle the tour group for a few seconds. You feel a burst of intense yet safe heat, but in an instant flare, Joan's terror becomes palpable. I walked the path Joan's tumbrel rolled from her prison cell to the stake in the marketplace and saw the cross that commemorates her sacrifice. It is a quiet and profound place; no one speaks above a whisper. Last, I looked at art dedicated to Joan of Arc, some of it in France, like the mosaic of Joan in the Sacré-Coeur in Paris and many pieces by artists from other times and places. Joan has inspired painters, sculptors, and multitudes of writers to render her for posterity, to make her immortal.

All my books deal in one manner or another with girl empowerment or lack thereof, and I often shape my heroines to challenge gender bias and oppression in different periods of history. Joan of Arc, however, is an interesting case. Although she has become a symbol of female strength, she would not have seen herself like that. She would have seen herself as simply doing what was required, not making a statement about gender identity or empowerment or women's role in society. She was following a mission from God. In her eyes, she could just as easily have been a boy and accomplished what she did. Role models, however, become who and what we need them to be to better the world we live in now. And Joan *was* a girl. Six hundred years after her death, we are still starved for stories of girls who have accomplished greatness, because there remains an imbalance in the historical record.

Joan of Arc's renown spans continents, cultures, and centuries. I'm not sure if it's an entirely positive thing that most people can name only one female warrior in over six hundred years, and some people have never even heard of Joan. Can you name another girl who saved her nation who wasn't born a queen? I find it sad that the most famous historical role model for teenage girls lived so long ago. I do not believe Joan should be that much of a phenomenon. Yet she is. And she is often considered miraculous, not just unique.

In recent years, much awareness and long-overdue attention has been paid to speaking one's truth, to standing up to harassment and bullying and abuse. Joan dealt with discrimination and harassment over six hundred years ago. Somehow, she bucked convention and accomplished great things. But it cost Joan her life.

This generation has embraced and championed awareness. Joan found a way to action. Combine awareness and action without repercussion and there is not only forward movement, but a tectonic shift. Imagine a girl who makes history and lives. I want to write a book about her next. Or if not me, then I hope that someone who is reading this will.

JEHANNE AND THE HUNDRED YEARS' WAR

In writing historical fiction you have to make choices, and in this book I elected to spell Joan of Arc's name as she signed it, Jehanne. The French spelling of Joan is often Jeanne, and in her childhood, Joan was sometimes referred to as Jeannette. But the name she chose to call herself was Jehanne.

Jehanne grew up during a chaotic period in French history. Her country was not only at war with England but also engaged in a civil war. In the past, all the regions of France had clearly supported the same sovereign as the king of their country; only the English had contested it. But in Jehanne's time a large portion of the French populace supported the English king as the king of France, while others backed the son of the previous French king.

The area of France where Jehanne was born fell largely under the control of the French Burgundians, who had allied themselves with England. But Jehanne lived in a village under the fiefdom of the one major city in the northeast territory, Vaucouleurs, that aligned itself with the opposition, the Armagnacs. The Armagnacs fought against having the English king, Henry VI, on the throne of France. They firmly believed the French dauphin, Charles, was France's rightful sovereign. Unfortunately, in 1428, when Jehanne entered the scene, her side was losing badly, and it appeared the leader she supported, the dauphin Charles, might give up the fight entirely.

Jehanne knew a country that had experienced almost eighty years of warfare. Although the Hundred Years' War has a long and complicated history, to fully understand the world that she inhabited, it's helpful to look at how and why the war between England and France began. Jehanne would have known this history. The battles likely inspired her to want to effect change.

In the fourteenth and fifteenth centuries, it was a great prize to sit on the French throne. France had the largest population in Europe, and its ruler could amass vast armies and tap enormous fiscal resources. So when the French king Charles IV died in 1328 without sons, Edward III, the king of England, Duke of Guyenne (part of Aquitaine in southwestern France), and Charles IV's cousin, felt he had a legitimate claim to the French throne. The other competitor to be king of France was the Count of Valois, Philip VI, a grandson of a previous king of France, Philip III.

The French assembly chose Philip VI to be king of France. At first Edward III accepted the decision and was satisfied to retain his land in France. However, Philip VI feared another king's power in his dominion and tried to remove England altogether from France, so Edward III renewed his claim to the French throne. And thus, in 1337, began the Hundred Years' War.

At the beginning of the war, English armies kept the French on the defensive. Yet even though England consistently won battles, the English failed to expand their area of occupation.

Then in 1356, they captured John II, the latest king of France. Treaties were negotiated granting England full sovereignty over its French territories, and in return the king of France would be released. Unfortunately, John II died in an English prison. And the conflict over the French crown began anew.

This time the French king Charles V put the English on the defensive, and the English lost almost all their holdings in France. When Charles V died in 1380, the English retained only the port of Calais and a few other coastal cities.

In 1380, the period before Jehanne emerged on the scene, Charles VI was crowned king of France. Because he was only eleven, his uncles acted as his regents. It was their job collectively to run the government, yet only one uncle, Duke Philip the Bold of Burgundy, set the young king's policy. When Charles VI came of ruling age, he and the French populace were fed up with his uncle's self-serving policies and high taxes. After decades of fighting, the war had become very unpopular with the peasants in both countries because of the high taxes required to sustain it. Charles reformed the government and earned his people's love. They called him the Beloved King.

However, in 1392, Charles VI began to suffer from bouts of what we would now recognize as paranoid schizophrenia. For the rest of his reign, he became known as the Mad King. France once again fell into a regency, only this time an open conflict over control of king and country ensued between the king's uncle Philip the Bold, the Duke of Burgundy, and the king's brother, Louis I, the Duke of Orléans.

Fortunately for France, England was incapable of renewing war at the time.

Philip the Bold died in 1404, but the battle over control of the Mad King continued. Unlike his father, the new Duke of Burgundy, John the Fearless, had no close personal relationship with King Charles VI. He found himself outmaneuvered politically, so in 1407 he arranged for the assassination of the Duke of Orléans. His involvement in the murder was quickly revealed. Angered and horrified by John's treachery, Bernard VII of Armagnac took up the Duke of Orléans's cause. Civil war raged between the Armagnacs (supporters of the dead Duke of Orléans and, later, proponents of the son of the Mad King, the dauphin Charles) and the Burgundians. Regions and cities across France chose sides.

The new English king, Henry V, saw an opportunity amidst all the French discord. A worthy general as well as a powerful king, Henry invaded France in 1415. At the Battle of Agincourt, Henry's army killed nearly half of the French nobility. By the end of Henry V's campaign, England ruled the entire region of Normandy for the first time in two centuries.

The civil war between the Burgundians and the Armagnacs escalated. In retaliation for John's murder of the Duke of Orléans, John the Fearless himself was assassinated, and the dauphin Charles was implicated in the plot. The Burgundians seized Paris in 1419, and the dauphin was forced to flee south into Armagnac territory. Angered by his father's assassination, the newest Duke of Burgundy, Philip the Good, encouraged the king of England, Henry V, to claim the French throne. An alliance formed between England and Burgundy.

In the 1420 Treaty of Troyes, Mad Charles VI, who was still officially the king of France, set aside his own son, the dauphin, and ceded the right of succession to Henry V. The Mad King also married his daughter Catherine to Henry V, strengthening Henry's claim to the French throne. Henry's heirs would now legitimately rule both France and England.

But then English good fortune turned to dust. Henry V and Charles VI died within weeks of each other in 1422. And the infant Henry VI of England became king of two lands.

However, Charles VI's son, the dauphin, would not easily relinquish his inheritance. The dauphin knew he still retained the allegiance of the larger part of France. But because he was incapable himself of military leadership, he hoped to reconcile with the Duke of Burgundy.

Jehanne d'Arc appeared and sparked a revival of French morale. The French began winning battles, and the tide turned against the English. This led to the dauphin's coronation in July 1429. He became Charles VII, the anointed King of France.

The Duke of Burgundy switched his allegiance, and Paris and all of Normandy once again came under the authority of Charles VII and France.

When the English lost the minor Battle of Castillon in 1453, according to history books the Hundred Years' War ended. Yet no treaty was concluded, and skirmishes would recur for many years to come. At the end of the war, the English would retain only the city of Calais. And France, now a proudly unified nation, intended to stay that way.

The Hundred Years' War remains the longest military conflict in European history.

FRENCH AND ENGLISH MONARCHS

Charles IV the Fair (Charles IV le Bel) *January 3, 1322–February 1, 1328* (king of France prior to war; his death started the dispute over the French throne)

<u>KINGS OF FRANCE DURING THE HUNDRED YEARS' WAR</u>
Philip VI of Valois the Fortunate (Philippe VI de Valois, le Fortuné) *April 1, 1328–August 22, 1350*

John II the Good (Jean II le Bon) *August 22, 1350–April 8, 1364*

Charles V the Wise (Charles V le Sage) *April 8, 1364–September 16, 1380*

Charles VI the Beloved, the Mad (Charles VI le Bienaimé, le Fol) *Septempber 16, 1380–October 21, 1422*
Jehanne was born in 1412, when Charles VI was forty-three.

Charles VII the Victorious, the Well-Served (Charles VII le Victorieux, le Bien-Servi) *October 21, 1422–July 22, 1461*

Jehanne was ten when Charles VI died in 1422, and when Charles VII should have been crowned king.

Jehanne was seventeen at Charles VII's coronation in 1429. She died in 1431, before he came to sit on the throne and rule all of France.

KINGS OF ENGLAND DURING THE HUNDRED YEARS' WAR

Edward III (House of Plantagenet) *January 25, 1327–June 21, 1377*

Richard II (House of Plantagenet) *June 22, 1377– September 30, 1399*

Henry IV, Henry of Bolingbroke (House of Lancaster) *September 30, 1399–March 20, 1413*

Henry IV ruled England during the first year of Jehanne's life.

Henry V (House of Lancaster) *March 20, 1413–August 31, 1422*

During Jehanne's childhood, ages two through ten, Henry V ruled England, acquired a large portion of France, and called himself the king of France.

Henry VI (House of Lancaster) *September 1, 1422– March 4, 1461*

Jehanne was ten when the six-month old baby Henry VI became king of England and France. She spent the last years of her life (1428–1431) trying to remove him from France. Henry would have been only nine at the time of her death.

SHOULD YOU WISH TO EXPLORE FURTHER

BOOKS

Belloc, Hilaire. *Joan of Arc*. First published 1930 by Little, Brown and Company (Boston). Milwaukee: Cavalier Books, 2014.

Brooks, Polly Schoyer. *Beyond the Myth: The Story of Joan of Arc*. Boston: Houghton Mifflin Company, 1990.

Castor, Helen. *Joan of Arc: A History*. New York: Harper Perennial, 2015.

Funck-Bretano, F. *Joan of Arc*. Trans. Madame Régis Michaud. First published 1912. Mineola, New York: Calla Editions, 2016.

Girault, Pierre-Gilles. *Joan of Arc*. Paris: Éditions Jean-Paul Gisserot, 2013.

Goldstone, Nancy. *The Maid and the Queen: The Secret History of Joan of Arc*. New York: Penguin Books, 2012.

Gordon, Mary. *Joan of Arc: A Life*. New York: Penguin Books, 2000.

Gower, Ronald Sutherland. *Joan of Arc*. 1893. Reprint, London: Pantianos Classics, 2017.

Harrison, Kathryn. *Joan of Arc: A Life Transfigured*. New York: Doubleday, 2014.

Hobbins, Daniel, trans. *The Trial of Joan of Arc*. Cambridge: Harvard University Press, 2005.

Kudlinski, Kathleen. *Joan of Arc*. New York: DK Publishing, 2008.

Pernoud, Régine. *Joan of Arc: By Herself and Her Witnesses*. Trans. Edward Hyams. First published in the French language in 1962 by Editions du Seuil. Lanham, Maryland: Scarborough House, 1994.

Sibout, Cécile-Anne. *Joan of Arc and Rouen*. Trans. Hazel Bertrand. Rouen, France: Éditions des Falaises, 2015.

Wilkinson, Philip. *Joan of Arc: The Teenager Who Saved Her Nation*. Washington, DC: National Geographic Society, 2007.

WEBSITES AND LOCATIONS

Historial Jeanne d'Arc: www.historial-jeannedarc.fr
   7 rue Saint-Romain, 76000 Rouen, France
Rouen 1431 360° Panorama: www.panoramaxxl.com
   14 bis avenue Pasteur, 76006 Rouen

ACKNOWLEDGMENTS

Many thanks to my home team, without whom this book would fail to exist: my parents, sister, and Craig, who read the terrible early drafts and the down-to-the-wire deadline drafts; my invaluable writing group of Penny Blubaugh, Candace Fleming, and Barb Rosenstock, who transform my words into a story worth reading; and Lorie Ann Grover, who encouraged me when I needed it most. Steve Malk, there are not enough words of gratitude—thank you for your friendship and guidance and for always believing in my books. But as is often the case, if anything works in this novel, it is because of Alessandra Balzer. Without her insights and inspiration Joan of Arc would have remained entombed in history. Any life breathed into *The Language of Fire* was because of a great editor.

STEPHANIE HEMPHILL

is the award-winning author of *Hideous Love: The Story of the Girl Who Wrote Frankenstein*; *Wicked Girls: A Novel of the Salem Witch Trials*, a *Los Angeles Times* Book Prize finalist; *Your Own, Sylvia: A Verse Portrait of Sylvia Plath*, a Michael L. Printz Honor Book; *Sisters of Glass*; and *Things Left Unsaid: A Novel in Poems*. She lives in Chicago.

Follow Stephanie Hemphill on